SON OF THE SAVANNAH

BY

DR. ALHASAN SISAWO CEESAY, MD

FIRST PRINTING

PUBLISH KUNSA.COM

ISBN 978-1-910117-89-7

INSCRIBED TO

My Parents, Wife and Children, Teachers, Friends,
Colchester Friends of Manding Charitable Trust UK and
Friends of Manding Alpena, Michigan, USA and the
downtrodden.

Africans must now start documenting courageous Heroes
as well as unusual achievements made in the days of
yore.

Dr. Alhasan S. Ceesay, MD

PREFACE AND ACKNOWLEDGMENTS

No knowledge is gained without hard work and patients. We all need small challenge in one form or the other, or degradation to appreciate life and our environment. This work tells of a moving and spellbinding story of Kunsa Badibunka, a twin born and breadth in the savannah, and his travels to Guinea Conakry to wed his bride Fanta Kurung. In guinea Kunsa found a magnificent, sensual, ecstatic romantic experience in Fanta Kurung.

The characters depicted represent no real people or anyone in particular; even if these may coincidentally be identical to someone a reader may know or identify with. All efforts are in place to avoid revealing the actual people or those with similar experience akin to Kunsa's.

Besides providing vivid knowledge of the savannah Kunsa's tenacity to travel on foot to region thousands of miles full of Lions, Hyenas, Wilder beasts, Elephants, and Giraffes just to name a few, was feat boys of his days dream of. Kunsa Badibunka was West Africa's unknown explorer and this work is to document that trail.

Kunsa is West Africa's blazing combination of Marco Polo and Sinbad the sailor. In the mean time allow me express profound gratitude to my wife Mrs. Fatou Koma Ceesay and our children: Famatanding Ceesay, Binta Ceesay and Roheyata Ceesay for bearing and persevering patiently through with me in thick and thin during my drive to bring the Golden Flees of medical aid and service to villagers.

Also I am immensely thankful to illustrious lawyer Ousainu Darboe and the following, Lorna Robinson, Eliza Jones, Dr. Laurel Spooner, Dr. Barbra Murray, Dr. Phil Spooner, Dr. Richard Murray, Dr. Malkaight Singh, Cloyd Ramsey, Howard Riggs, Rita Riggs, Dr. Charles Egli, Dr. Cooper Milner, Dr. Nelson Herron, Deidre O'Leary, Margaret Cruise, Bill Cruise, Alison Cruise, Dr. Eunice Kahan, Dr. Betzabi Alison-Prager, Henry Valli, Fr. John Milner, Homer Sheppard, Geraldine Sheppard, Dr. Ebrahima Malick Samba, Keba Sanneh, Matida Sanneh, Hon. Amang Kanyi, Dr. Lamin J. Sise B, Dr. Sulayman S. Nyang, Bishops Masson & Coleman McGhee of the Episcopal Diocese of Michigan, Detroit, the Ceesay Committee Diocese of Michigan, Lois R. Leonard, Rev. Walter White, Rev Huge White, Patricia Koblynski, Ishfaue Ahmed, Imran Khurum Ahmed, Mohamed Nasir, Ahmed Nizami, Abdinnisir Hassan, Faisal Alim, Abdal Rhaseed Suguelle, Noora Sugulle, Mahmud Adam, Ganem Al Haidard, Abdullah Shahim, Asiya Qadri, Yusuf Ali, Dr.

Haidar Salih and numerous others whose names are not mention but not forgotten. I write to raise money for the building of a village hospital at Njawara, the Gambia. It is my hope that you would be inspired to join our dream of providing medical aid and service to Gambian villagers and children in the North Bank region.

Purchasing this book or donating in cash or kind would help bring our dream to fruition of Manding Medical Centre for a much needed healthcare delivery and hope to villagers, especially children who frequently die prematurely from childhood diseases because of lack of medical service.

Together we can catch a dream for the villager and children. Log onto: www. Friends of Manding gambimed, to learn more about our self-help village health project Manding Medical Centre at Njawara. Portions of proceed from sale of this work go to support goals of Manding Medical Centre.

In addition it will in due course offer scholarships to rural candidates wishing to read for a medical or an agricultural degree and return to serve in rural Gambia.

Dr. Alhasan S. Ceesay, MD

Chapter 1

Panyeki Village

Kunsa Badibunka was one of male twins born to Sisawo Badibunka and Famata Sherifo Tarawaleh at Panyeki village. From the day Kunsa was able walk he showed signs of an adventurer. Kunsa would leave his docile twin partner at home and walk three miles into snake, hyenas and cheetah infested bush to the fields on the other side of Panyeki village.

Home, sweet home is place that resonates with our historical birth. First let us note that Panyeki is still nestled between Suware Kunda and Nfamori Kunda villages in the Lower Badibou District at the North Bank of the Gambia.

Historically Panyeki had never exceeded beyond three thousands inhabitants all of who are grass root farmers. It was founded by rebellious Grandpa Bajo Badibunka who had a beef with then chief Sefo Njanko Kinteh.

At Panyeki the night choir consist of braying of donkeys intermingled with sporadic howls of hyenas. Panyeki itself is a collection of mud huts built about in open spaces with no fencing around them. Smoke bellows from more than half a dozen huts masking part of the early morning sunrise.

Son of the Savannah

There are no real streets but alley ways or footpaths leading to and from one hut to another. The time clocks are cocks ushering dawn intermingled with the call of morning prayers.

Panyeki lack's modern-day amities such as electricity, safe drinking water and block or buildings made of breaks, good infrastructure, and there were neither cars nor Lories plying the streets. Only horse or donkey drawn carts transport goods and people.

To outsiders Panyeki was just a simple grass-filled village where kids, under watchful eyes of grandparents, play happily the game of hide and seek in between trees while jumping over snakes, scorpions and at times almost falling into very deep abandon wells.

The People of Panyeki simply put, are ordinary farmers, who never heard of tractors or combine harvesters nor can they ever afford or operate these had they been made available to them.

These farmers were contended and very happy with the cutlasses, machetes, hoes or local plough called 'Drambo' and tools passed onto them by their great, great, great grandparents as farming tools. With these they used them to feed, support and defend their families and properties.

The social life was communal where what affected one affects all. Marriages, christenings and deaths were equally attended and contributed to by all within the village and the surrounding hamlets. Panyeki was your typical Gambia village of cheer and hard work being the only rewarding social welfare system.

Our adventurer Kunsa Badibunka and playmates knew every inch of the village. Here kids do not question parents and teachers but do as commanded. In Panyeki there is a code of conduct which strictly observes custom, family, tradition, and communal life.

The bush becomes the classroom and art of survival being learnt by observing what elders and especially your family does to overcome challenges of responsibilities along with those sad surprises that natural catastrophes unveils.

People wore beautiful light dress made mostly of cotton and other fibres they can soften and weave into sheets to make dresses out of. Some of the embroidery is unique and intricate.

Panyeki is microcosm of the Gambia for inhabiting her are Mandinkas, Fulas, Wolof, Sereres, Mansuwankas, konyaginkas, and my palm wine kandabo friends the Jola tribes along with a few Serra Leoneans and Liberians.

Son of the Savannah

I hope this has given you a bird's eye view of Panyeki the birth home of our hero and adventurer Kunsa Badibunka. It is a pulsating village tradition depicting movers and sages and how rural knowledge and tribal cohesiveness are maintained and passed to next generations.

We will travel the path of young and ambitious Kunsa Badibunka quenches his thirst for knowledge and will to share his accruements with his people.

Dr. Alhasan Ceesay and Sisawo Ceesay, Dad 1960

Chapter 2

Boyhood Days

Youth makes most of us want to question and to conquer. So was it for Kunsa Badibunka. He was endowed with prowess, brilliance and wit sharper than any of his compatriots. And yet he exhibited the most humble and simplicity that made him the endeared to nearly all in Panyeki and the surrounding hamlets.

Kunsa Badibunka epitomized rituals and his imbibing of high fidelity ancestral values and virtues made him very unique. His fame literally overshadowed, Hussein Badibunka, his twin partner, who he defends with his life against very cruel and strong bullies of his day. Kunsa does best at what village male youths do.

He became a wrestler that harvested endless village champion trophies of the Badibous. Yes, the girls vied and sang his name in prose and poetry and were ready to sell their grannies and aunts to earn a wink from Kunsa Badibunka.

No tale about the Mandinkas would do justice in absence of the annual grand festivities and wrestling that takes place at the village open hall, called the Bantaba. Here is Panyeki's way of marking the grand occasion of the farmers' year.

Son of the Savannah

Societies and communities since the arrival of Adam and Eve to mother earth have designated a day or special week in which to pay homage or express gratitude to what they took for granted and referred as Supreme Being for being kind and having seen them through the previous year and its challenges.

In the Mandinka tradition, Mansa Bengo takes place annually after the harvest. On this day every villager in his or her best attire, queen, king and dancers gather in one large village for a week or two weeks long celebration and thanks giving.

The festivities are marked by dancing, music, magic, acrobatics, wrestling and abundant free food and drinks for every attendant. Normally, word is sent out early in the year, well before the festivities, for the wrestlers and other contestants to prepare them for the challenge.

Great competition exists between villages until the end of the grand festivities. Each contesting village wants their representative to be crowned that years' champion. The most lucrative rewards go to the wrestler who finally ends up champion over the rest.

The contest is divided into three categories thus: welterweight, middleweight and supper sized wrestlers. Show starts on the second day with the welterweights battling it out. The winners of that level go into a semi final two days later.

Next follows the middleweight who sought themselves in manner similar to those of the welterweight group. Winners continue to the final grand wrestling day. The biggest battle is waged with supper sized heavy wrestlers.

Theirs go to the wee hours of the night before final winners emerges to contest for the crown or trophy at the end of the festivities. Almost always a surprise winner proceeds to the next phase emerges.

Prices are offered for all categories on the final day. The welterweight champion likewise that of the middle weight are normally given specially embroiled trousers and trophies but not as high quality as that the heavy weight champion gets nor are they entitled to the privileges accompanying being victor of the heavy weights.

These not only get trophies, money or animals, super decorated embroiled trouser but they are privileged by tradition to have to choose the most beautiful single dame of the gathering to be their future wife.

Hence young twenty years old ladies try their best in looking presentable and beautiful so that the champion selects them. It is pride and honor if their dreams come true by being chosen by the champion of the day.

The physique and strength of the winner is something that entices women. They dream to have children for such super humans and so they pray that a champion from Senegal, Morocco, Sera Leon, Ghana, Mali, and Badibou select them.

Son of the Savannah

All the neighboring villages send in dancers, acrobats, poets, singers, soloist, and poets along with their medicine men, commonly known as voodoo men in your neck of woods. Yes, the medicine man served two purposes for his amulet are accepted as strength providers and also it wards off the powers emanating from the opposing camp.

Believe can be delusional but stands unique until proven illogical. None other than following principals, Sefo Fafanding Kinte and the Alkalo crowns the champion of the day, which alone is a cherished honor never to be forgotten by the recipient.

The festivities normally come to close on a Friday night. It is commonly referred to as the jubilant night and drumming, dancing and singing goes on throughout the night to near midday on following Saturday before everyone finally heads home to repose.

Both attendants and wrestler return home contended. Every event takes in a disciplined manner and most admirable fashion. Legend has it that our Kunsa Badibunka worn not only two or three but three dozen village annual wrestling champion crowning.

The contestants go home happy that they were able to participate and enjoy themselves while entertaining and keeping the Mandinka Mansa Bengo tradition alive. The crowning of the champion is ceremony of vital exercise in Mandinka tradition and scribes mark the occasion with historical chants about previous champion's generations past. Hearing this curdles the blood and draws ones' sinew to action. It is moving and full of pride and cultural history of Mandinkas.

Previous champions and the old or retired wrestlers open up the show by dancing and showing off their muscles and how they brought their opponent tumbling to the ground like a heavy log.

Many chiefs and mayors/village heads are invited to the ceremony, which lasts two days during which one of the Alkalo of Panyeki crowns the recent victor, and gives presents to the lady selected as his bride. With dignitaries and guest assembled the chief priest is asked to open the affair with prayers.

This is followed by throngs of colourfully dressed dancers from each of several villages performing their unique version to entertain and mark the historic nature of the Mandinka day.

Such festivity goes on until late in the evening before the drums and dancing temporally yield place for the audience to hear the Alkalo's speech along with that from some invited dignitary. Hence, at the end of all prerequisite formalities the Alkalo of Panyeki calls the new champion and the former to stand in the centre of the square and be recognized as winner and strength of the Badibous. The pages of the Alkalo carry with them bags of money, gold and lady the day's champion chose to wed joins them.

Strangely, Kunsa Badibunka had always declined the lady on grounds that he had other very important things to accomplish before marrying. Scribes chant songs that proclaim Mandinka history and tradition eons of the tribe's life.

The Alkalo, along with loads of presents from the state and visiting dignitaries, hands over the supper embroiled trouser to the victor of the day. He wears it and is also declared ambassador of congeniality for the state and travels to many nation exposing the values of sports and friendship it builds among nations and tribes.

The ceremony turn to the phase were the chief priest and his assistants joining the Panyeki Alkalo, champion and bride to bless the two in marriage? The bride and bridegroom head to unknown quarters for their honeymoon. The festivity continues and now takes an even more festive form commemorating the union of the champion and his bride. His peers from all villages give out money, presents and carvings to put a special seal to the marriage. Hence, dear reader, you can see why men struggle hard to become champion amongst these unique traditional achievers. The Mansa Bengo Champion!

Chapter 3

In pursuit of the Golden Flees

If ambition makes the man then the will to see it through is most admirable and fulfilling. Kunsa Badibunka has set his eyes to something much more worthy than a few accolades. Recall that in Kunsa's days there were only horses and donkeys used in travels.

Most of the travelling was done under very dangerous and challenging circumstances by foot and took months to get from point A to B of intended destinations. Kunsa started this one of a kind feat from the eastern banks of the River Gambia where he walked through thick canopy of vegetation and at times in almost tropical forest like wood full of vines intertwining and blocking his path.

All he has was his trusted sharp machete and a blanket to keep him warm at night. In the tree lurk uncompromising neck-breaking cheetahs. Not a single hair of Kunsa rose in fear of these for he was very certain of killing any that chose to surprise him.

He hacked his way for three days before reaching a hamlet where the inhabitant not only adore him but received him as their king. He decided to take a need rest and because of love the people had for Kunsa a hasty meeting was arranged for all to meet at the village Bantaba.

Son of the Savannah

The village crier announced that, "The visitor and king had some important proclamation to make before proceeding." At the Bantaba meeting and after everyone was seated venerable Kunsa Badibunka got up and walked to the centre of the Bantaba, after the Griots chanting of historical feats his great grand ancestors achieved along with his own, and said; "Fellow citizens and brave ones, I am overwhelmed by your generosity and humbled by your offer of crowning me King of Sare Boido.

It is an honor I will cherish for the rest of my life however I must move on to answers the call for all of us. I ask for your prayers and rest assured I will pass by some day with even more cheerful rewards to all. With this I seek your permit that I leave for my destination by dawn today. Thank you God bless and prosperous in good health."

The huge crowd on hearing his request went dead silent and it was the Alkalo who eventually mustered courage and strength and rose to offer a response. No one wanted Kunsa Babunka to go because of love they had for him and danger awaiting his next move.

With gut twisting the Alkalo cleared his throat and said, "My fellow villagers you have heard what is asked of us. I for one do not approve being aware of number of people who lost their lives trying to cross these uncharted fronts our new king intends to cross. I am certain speak loud and clear in your behalf for him to reconsider his life and good it would do rather than giving it up so prematurely.

We are sons of the Savannah and are fully aware of what lurks behind in these thick vegetation and trees. Has he not heard of the cheetahs and roaming lions that strewn path he is about to venture into?" The crowd acknowledged and confirmed the danger in unison.

The Alkalo continued saying "I do not want my final days be marked by sad disappearance of Badibu's hero. Thank you and that is all from me." This was followed by a lot of pandemonium for a while before the grand priest took his chance and turn to put sense in mind of the young hero he believed was about to end his life.

The priest; as usual of Mandnka gatherings, started by offering prayer for the safety and wellbeing of all. He said; "My king and indeed my son, risk you are about to take warrants me put this little bit of caution.

Of the many who ventured beyond this village never saw the dawn of the new day. The either are mewled by marauding hyenas, cheetahs or swallowed by humongous pythons waiting for such easy victims. The thought of falling into such an end pains our hearts. Again Sare Boido and all the representative of the neighboring hamlets urge you not waste your life in name of valor."

He then walked to Kunsa and embraced him for while before heading back to his seat. The last of the protest was an elderly man said to be the oldest in the region. He walked his very slowly with stick in hand to help his gait.

On getting close he greeted his hero and in tears begged, "Would your majesty heed the wishes of the people and stay alive? We will do anything to keep you happy for the rest of your life on cancelling this risky trip you are about to take. The oracle I consulted is dead against your venturing out this village and we agree with that request.

Son I implore not to go. Stay with ones that love and not one that would gladly feed upon your youthful flesh." Kunsa badibubka helped the old man to his seat and again reiterated that neither fear mongering nor lions on his path will stop him from his journey.

He thanked them and by dawn the village had lined up his path in tear to bid him farewell and bon chance knowing that none of them can stop the lionhearted Kunsa. With machete and black in addition to food ladies of Sare Boido prepared for him venerable and hero Kunsa took to the thick canopy clearing his way.

This time thing turned nasty and rough a few hundred kilometers from Sare Boido. Here he ran into a park of very hungry ferocious hyena and they were not going to him pass without them feeding upon his carcasses.

The howling almost deafened Kunsa but one thing helped. He was very steady and never showed any fear and day light was a few hours away. He knowing that he could fight these dozens of wild and hungry hyenas managed to climb on big Baobab tree and sit tight at the top until sunrise.

Son of the Savannah

Meanwhile the people at Sare Boido had given up and offered prayer for the soul of their king to have a resting place in death. Not Kunsa Badibunka, for at sunrise and with hyenas gone he chance his way again.

Only this time a huge snake ten times his size and five hundred yards long drag itself towards him. Kunsa quickly decided to place raw meat he had been carrying at the end of a big log and pushed it towards the nose of beast.

It luckily took the bait and swallowed both thorny log and meats at one go. This allowed Kunsa to jump over it and get going fast. It is known fact that once a big snake eats it movements are slowed.

Was it Kunsa's lucky star that shone on this occasion only time and history will tell but he escaped the region's most feared snake through simple ingenuity. Food he brought being exhausted he starting feeding on leaves berries, fruits such as wild mangoes, and a variety of edible root and tubers. Ill-luck came his way when he accidentally ate a very deceptive bright red looking enticing fruit.

He developed instant diarrhea and vomiting a few hours after consuming the fruit. Again our survivor found a safe cave to stay until he feels better. It would take three days before he could venture on his feet after having gathered strength. From hence forth he took great care about what he must consume no matter how hungry he may be.

Son of the Savannah

Back on the trail and after seven days of nonstop walk he came across a vast grassy clearing. Unknown to him he now has treaded in home of the King of the jungle. What surprised him most was the presence of a huge number of deer and Antelopes intermingled with Wildebeests.

He could not believe his fortune for he had travelled for days without eating flesh now he has an abundance of roaming a stone throw from him. He never thought this to be right place for lions to hunt. They had just eaten two Wildebeests on the day of his arrival and so were not yet concerned or interested to feed upon him.

Kunsa made a bow and arrow out of tree branches and short himself a priced male dear and later an Antelope. Using dried wood and grass he soon made the greatest fir upon which he roasted his kill. He gorged upon it for two days before hell broke loose. A three month mother lioness smelt his and burning meat and was soon growling a few feet from him.

He stayed still and did not move a muscle. With this docile attitude the Lioness too sat watching move Kunsa would do. The hunter and hunted remained calm but ready at any time to pounce to kill or survive. Soon the alpha male lion arrived heading towards Kunsa. The confrontation was tense as the king stood and looked directly at motionless kunsa Badindinka.

Dr. Alhasan Sisawo Ceesay, MD

The lucky thing for Kunsa Badibunka none of these lions were hungry but got drawn to him because of the smell emanating from his barbeques. However the alpha lion was not going to stop at just smelling or looking at Kunsa. It made few attacking gestures which were followed by springing suddenly towards Kunsa.

Kunsa ducked and noticed that only the male was attacking him. He thrust his sharp bladed long knife into the chest of the beast of forest rendering it instantly immobile. As miracle or luck will have it for Kunsa the female lioness walked away from the warring scenery and disappeared into the bush.

Having vanquished the alpha male lion Kunsa decided to push forward away from another surprise visit from female lions as these are more ferocious hunters that kill faster than male lions. It took another month of walking in thick vegetation before Kunsa Badibunka arrived at the boarder leading to Kundara in the Futajalong highlands.

At Kedugou village Kunsa decided to spend the rainy season for the trail he is about to take to Kundara is mountainous and full of deed valleys were many adventurers' corpses are found. The slightest slippage one does one finds oneself at the bottom of the deepest abyss. People always offer the last rights for those venturing to make the journey to Kundara.

Son of the Savannah

Kunsa found out that despite the abundance of natural food sources at Kedugou because of extreme poverty one comes across skeleton-like people. There was no need for these floods of hungry people had they organized themselves and till the land. Soon Kunsa organized a farmer's cooperative and battering unit for Keduguo.

It was so successful that other hamlets emulated it and crowning Kunsa as their Paramount chief. This initiative forced Kunsa to delay his venture for another year before bidding farewell to his beloved friends at Kedugou. He again refused wife the village offered him because mission he look to complete.

As the saying goes good things do not last long. Soon Kunsa Badibunka would park his skimpy belongings and move on towards Kundara at the Futajalong highlands. The village accompanied him until at the base of steep mountain Kunsa most scale before Kundara and there they prayed fervently and wished him goodbye fearing that he too would be among the corpses at the bottom of the gorge.

This part of Kunsa's adventure would crown testament of human endurance and determination to do good. Kunsa lost his footing a few kilometers up the terrain but luckily he held firm to branch of nearby tree preventing him from tumbling into dark snake filled whole. He was not discouraged but bravely continued the steep climb.

Dr. Alhasan Sisawo Ceesay, MD

These hills are said to be two thousand feet above sea level and on looking down at the bottom things people and nearby animals look like toys. Such was height Kunsa has to conquered before setting foot on flat ground two thousand miles from nearest village of his destination.

He believed cowards die twice before their own time and was not going to heed fear or scare mongering hungry villagers he just left behind. He was only able to climb a mile before the sunset. He wisely chose to spend the night between two huge boulders so that he does not roll over in his to his doom.

The only danger he faced at this hotel of the heights is snakes and scorpions. The brave and faithful never worry about pending danger or consequence of their mission. All they are interested in is reaching the target and taking the Golden Flees back home with them.

Kunsa commenced the next day's journey almost crawling because of the steepness of the path he has to follow to Kundara. He had barely covered twenty kilometers before the sun set. The nights at such heights, despite it being in Africa can be very cold.

Some say with high winds the chill factor can go down to minus ten degrees centigrade just as in the desert at night. All Kunsa Badibuka had with him was a thick cotton woven blanket. It in some nights freezes on him but being young and health he always made it to the next day.

Son of the Savannah

It took him a month and half before reaching flat land. His feet were sore and tired and he looked skeletal. Legend has it that on his way to Labe in the Futajalong region he picked up a five kilogram pure gold nugget. On realizing what was revealed to him he wrapped it in his blanket and would place his head on top of it while asleep.

Traders and gold smiths at Labe offered huge sums of money to buy it but he only requested the gold smith to break the nugget into pieces and make a necklace for his future bride. This done he sold the remainder at even higher prices making him one of richest in the region. With his new cloud away from home made him more determined to return with the sort Golden Flees.

The son of the Savannah kept his modest and humbleness all through his stay at Labe. While at Labe he bought hundreds of heads of cattle, Camels, Goats, and three hundred sheep and had them taken for him to Panyeki village in Gambia.

With money and golden necklace Kunsa Badibunka proceeded towards Kandia some two thousand miles from Labe or Conakry capital city of Guinea Conakry. Riding upon the strong white Arabian horse he bought at Kambia Kunsa headed for kandia the next trading centre.

He had by now numerous followers and savants at his disposal. Beautiful women tend to his care and lo he felt in cloud nine but still yearn to meet one pleasing to his heart.

The entourage arrived at Kandia late at night and reposed at home of Kusmani Kurung, a priest. He had three wives who all brought food and milk for his company. Kunsa Badibunka was said to be wide mouthed upon gazing upon Miss Fanta Kurung, elder daughter of Kusmani Kurung and Njanke Turek his first wife.

Kunsa's heart became restless and enamored while his small brain whirled in desire. His eyes met with those of gorgeous Fanta Kurung and the later smiled and shyly looked at the floor, which was a normal gesture of local girl in love.

The local dames do not flirt in like manner to their city counter parts but displace dignity, respect, courtesy and obedience. There is legacy of one night stand with these girls for come from good homed guided by discipline, faith and self pride. In this case and event both Fanta Kurung and Kunsa Badibunka could not stop gazing and smiling at each other any time chance allows.

Thus enamored the visitor decided to stay a few more days in Kandia. In the meant time one observant savant volunteered to bell the cat by asking kunsa, "Is is she not ravishing and most fitting queen for you?" Kuna gave a broad smile that ran from ear to hear for he liked what he just heard from his trusted savant.

Kuna called the savant on the side and asked, "How or what do I need do to wed this beauty you just noticed. My heart flutters whenever she is around. I love her to the core of my heart and would pay all my wealth and gold to have hand in marriage." At that the savant replied, "That is no problem to accomplish for I know her father. My family use to plant crops during the rainy season for him. He recognized and greeted me on day of our arrival to Kandia.

If you so desire I will tell him of your wish and let you know his side of the dream. Note that only fathers can give their daughters away in marriage. Let us prayer and sleep over this goal. I will by noon meet kusmani Kurung and have private tet-a-tet about your heart's wish with regards to his Fanta Kurung."

Kunsa turned and twisted all night praying for arrival of dawn and sunrise so his message would reach kusman Koma and eventually Fanta kurung and her mother Njake Turek. Sure enough Kunsa called Dembo Nyajara, his trusted savant and urge him to hurry with assignment they discussed night before.

Dembo Nyajara at the strike of noon was at kusman Koma's side placating his way into his heart for his friend to woe his daughter Fanta Kurung. He began the conversation by reminding Kusmani how his family always remembers kindness Kusmani showed while they work at his farm. On being certain of having attention of Kusmani Dembo Nyajata opened up the floodgates of request from his friend and master Kunsa Badibunka.

Dembo Nyajara told Kusmani Kutung, "Sir, I am a messenger for one whose heart melted upon seeing your daughter. He is an honest, hard working person of faith that vowed to love and make your daughter Fanta Kurung happy if you would approve his marrying her before returning to Panyeki in the Gambia.

I can assure you that he is ready to any dowry you wished today. I can vouch to his richness as his attire and entourage should signal." Old man Kusmani Kurung listened intently and replied, "Leave matters in God's hands. Go and tell Kunsa Badibunka that my wife and me and relevant relatives would discourses his wish and will tell you our decision by noon tomorrow."

With this gleeful Dembo Nyajara ran to tell eager Kunsa Badibunka of the initial good news from the old man kusmani Kurung. Two days passed by without any news despite Dembo's visitations and having long chats with members of the Kurung family.

Mean while Fanta Kurung was sent to her Aunt twenty kilometers away while the family deliberates over her future. Sadly enough marrying girls or women never have chance to be part of the debate but only parents, relatives and long time trusted friends participate in such deliberations. I called it Africa's blind dating which can go either way depending upon the backgrounds of the couple.

Legend has it that, with blessings of Njake Turek and her husband Kusmani Kurung it had been agreed for the wedding to take place in a month's time at the grand mosque and festivity at the love Bantaba in Kandia the Guinea. This they kept the most guarded secrets from friends and media.

In the interim Fanta Kurung was told of the decision by her Aunt Madam Maraka Kurunga. The news left Fanta Kurung feeling like being in dreamland and hoped she woke up with the stars and the situation still real for them. Her sisters and girl friends supported and encourage each other during the preparation for the grandest occasion and cerebration of the region.

Fanta kurung avoided straying and from believing rumors from medium gimmickry. She promised to make the man who touched her heart with love have good future. All marveled and happily pray for prosperity and happy future for the couple.

Her best friend Amazoza told Fanta Kurung, "We assure you of our continued love and willingness to offer guidance any time you and Kunsa Badibunka needed it." With misty eyes Fanta Kurung apologized for all the bad things she might have done to the family and friends.

The two affirm their love for each other and hugged for ten minutes in-between sobs.

The tick of the old grandfather's clock was the only sound heard while the girls went into a silent prayer for their future. At this hour the well-meaning angel in both girls surfaced. The moment was so touching that only the heartless would remain unmoved.

They got up and walked hand in hand towards Kunsa Badibunka who did not disturb their solace. He smilingly held Fanta Kurung and said, "Darling it is time for your being away for a few more weeks and assured her that his life is woven around her."

Fanta Kurung secretly pinched herself to be certain that she was in real about to be wedded by not only a filthy rich male but one she loves to the care of her being. Never in her early life, whether in primary or high school life, did it occur to Fanta kurung that life would be this kind to her after college.

Yes, boys at one time or the other have made appreciable remarks about perfection and beauty of her features and facial presentation. Some admirers even dared to compare her with Rachael Welch and Marling Monroe of America.

Brother Dudou Ceesay, in green, with family, 1965

Son of the Savannah
Chapter 4
Turning into New leaf

However, Fanta Kurung now swore to use her newfound gift to be role model by displaying acceptable social attitudes and contributing positively to community they may find themselves. Fanta Kurung promised to set up a charity to help hungry people and drug addicts. Nurse Majula had already committed herself to helping Kunsa's self-help village health project flourish.

They are doing this with intense believe that they are their community's keeper and that the good we do on earth should not be buried or interred with our bones but should out live us for the benefit of generations to follow. They asked, "What was the use of money if one hoards it and turned a miser while others live in deprivation and hunger of no fault of theirs?

No, not creating free loafers but giving a helping hand to raise both spirit and efforts of the downtrodden to rise to better levels in this life. All able bodies should be able to work for descent life of their own and not be saddled under cloaks of ingenious welfare systems that only make them poorer in their self worth and income."

Kunsa Badibunk promised to start business in Panyeki, Senegal and Egypt in Africa. He hoped that over five thousand families will benefit from his African enterprises. He told Famta Kurung, "With you by my side they could guarantee help for even more poor villagers in Africa and the developing world.

Fanta Kurung affirmed and said, "I am a brand new born again lady and my old ways are in the past for good because I wanted to be loved and to belong to a good thing in this life." Kunsa Badibunka and Fanta kurung were happy that their lives were cemented not only for themselves but to be charitable to the needy.

With the above desire to turn into a new leaf in their minds the pair started to seriously reflect on when and where to be wedded. Princess Diana would envy the couple for there were no intrusion to their freedom by the media and paparazzi.

These cannot imagine how there was no freedom, human rights or even law or respect of the individual's right to be free of press harassment. Everyone, especially the press, wanted to make money off them and had daring minds to style them celebrity only because of the promised wealth combined with facial beauty.

Young girls are encouraged to be copycats, when their parents knew that the poor things would never look like Fanta Kurung or have the luck that surfaced for Fanta kurung. Some today called the paparazzi cameramen hooligans because of the deliberate ways they brandish cameras onto faces not resonating with such a wish or expectation of those being photographed.

Chapter 5
DATE OF THE WEDDING SET

Griot frenzy has now turned not only Kandia but also the entire region into state of an expectant society in painful gestation in anticipation of the region's biggest event. Aching for the mother of all weddings everyone wondered where it would take place, whether the wedding was going to be private and who would be on the official invitation list of that historic day of days for the region.

No one knew details of the wedding because the couple wanted to complete their preparations before letting the cat out of the bag. The plans were finally consummated at a family meeting held secretly in locality of Kandia away from the Griots. There the future couples agreed that the wedding would happen at the great Bantaba of lovers in kandia Guinea, Conakry, West Africa.

The occasion will be an interfaith officiating and all major religions will be represented and will offer prayers. It was agreed that the wedding take place on the first Friday after harvest to enable all villagers wanting to participate in the ceremony attend. A list of who is who not only in the Badibous and Guinea but also in the political arena was wisely drawn from spectrum of politicians.

The media started vying for locations and people to interview on the great day even though it would be a month before Fanta Kurung take her vows. The tabloids and various village organizations went into frenzy of preparation as to who would be most artistic and perform the most remembered feat of all dances. Neighboring villages in Gambia and Senegal cashed in and prepared to take the show on the day of days for the region.

Dr. Alhasan Sisawo Ceesay, MD
Chapter 6
MOTHER OF ALL WEDDINGS

The city of Kandia is an old colonial trading center and gateway to Conakry capital of Guinea. Kandia is thw second largest city and served as a vibrant trading post during colonial days. Both Kunsa Badibunk and Fanta Kurung are members of the Mandinka tribe whose great grandparents migrated from now Republic of Mali to the Badibous in the Gambia central region of Guinea Conakry.

Fanta kurung like all Mandinka girls was groomed, like their parents before them, to become good farmers and house wives. Their great, great, grandparents, unlike the break homes these girls live in, lived in huts and mud houses some distance away from the fields.

Kandia was then a rural village with few thousand inhabitants with no roads, only bush paths through thick savanna grass. It had an abundance of cattle, horses, goats and sheep grazing in the vacant fields.

Hence transformed Kandia has dramatically turned into the metropolitan city you are about to celebrate history of a magnificent wedding. The momentousness of the occasion left Fanta Kurung at lost in the welter of thousand details.

Every aspect was well orchestrated and her wedding dresses looked superb and admirable. Kusa Badibunka gladly paid for the bills and more. All was set by midday of Thursday twenty fours to wedding day. Young ladies in towns and villages wished their day to be half as historic and romantic as the one they are about to witness.

Son of the Savannah

Soon the Alice in wonderland wedding of prince and princess dawned. Mean while Kandia swelled to almost quarter of a million by the last week of the wedding. Buntings and flags flew all over the city as if it were going to have a coronation.

The Lovers' hall at Hotel De amour had a special facelift and a makeover with effigies of the ladies and their feature husbands on display. Security was beefed up well in advance of the ceremony for fear of trouble from competitors.

Friday, the day of the wedding, dawned bright and clear. kandia was turned into the largest gathering of happy, cheering, smiling, dancing villagers, and onlookers lining the streets to have a glimpse of the cars of the brides and bridegrooms. People in celebrant mood struggled with flags, buntings in hand to see the bridal cars.

It was not until after midday that the procession to Hotel de amour began with people cheering, throwing rice, flowers and even kisses at the bridal cars. The cars crawled towards the hall because of people eager or wanting to touch them or place their bouquet of flowers on them.

Finally the bridal entourage reached the hall and proud and happy father of the lady met the couple at the door and walked the isles to hand Fanta kurung over to take her vows gracefully.

Fanta Kurung was just radiant and charming to behold. On this lovely Friday Fanta Kurung and Kunsa Badibunka took their vows to be wedded to each other respectively. This was good omen for villagers who just had a bumper harvest added to this once in a life ceremony in behalf of one their own. The ceremony officiated by priests from all major denominations took full two hours before the married couples could stand at a special balcony erected for the purpose to thank those who in any way made it so warm and historic for them and kandia. They then joined VIPs and invited guests at the banquet hall for the reception.

From this formal reception the couple headed to the square at the center of the city, where the scene looked like a great sea of villagers, to witness the most colorful display of dance, acrobats, wrestling, and spectacular feat of magic performed by various groups and villages.

Yes, events of the wedding ceremony reverberated in every village and hamlet of the kandia.

The television, media and paparazzi had a field day and many people vied to be interviewed or photographed while hold pictures of the wedded. Kunsa Badibunka provide all the food, a dozen bulls were slaughter for the villagers to feast on.

The celebrations continued to the wee hours of the night before the people went to rest. It picked from where it ended on Friday right through Wednesday before the celebrants called it quit.

Kandia was overwhelmed with the sense of history and joy this wedding brought to it. The city will never be the same again for it will now be inundated with more tourists than it ever dreamt of. Mean while the married couple had left quietly to spend their honeymoon at an unknown location in Conakry.

They returned two weeks later with Fanta kurung heading to Panyeki Gambia. There Panyeki village reciprocated and threw in an unmatched bash for Kunsa and Fatou Kurung. Fanta Kurung set up an orphanage while Kunsa funded construction of a village hospital for his brother, who has just graduated from medical school, to run.

Dr. Alhasan Ceesay, Famatanding Tarawaleh, Babucar Diba, Penda Diba, Fatou Diba and Isatou Diba, Banjul, Gambia, 1965

Dr. Alhasan Sisawo Ceesay, MD
Chapter 7
Back in Gambia

The in-laws shuttled between Kindia and Panyeki t visit Kunsa and Fatou kurung. Kunsa Badibunka continued to give lavish presents of dresses, gold necklaces, and sailing trips aboard his local cruiser.

Kunsa badibunka wondered what the former colonial rulers did for the poor of the Gambia if such basic things like hospitals, good drinking water, schools, farming, and electricity hardly existed in these villages after three hundred plus years of ruling the country.

The most generous of kunsa Badibunka's contribution was helping Panyeki set up the children's hospital at the village medical center. He also provided scholarships and grants for those wishing to become nurses and doctors serving the center.

Such benevolence and success at his business propelled kunsa Badibunka to the envy of the Gambian Mafia, the most heinous group in West Africa. Soon he found dead fish thrown at his door with little threatening notes attached. The most serious requested him to hand over all his assets and businesses to the almighty Gambian Mafioso or he and his family would face severe retributions.

Kunsa's reporting this to the police accelerated action from the Mafia. They burnt one villa he loves to the ground and killed an uncle. This prompted Kunsa Badibunka to yield to their command and found his way to America under different pseudonyms. Meanwhile Fanta kurung returned to the Guinea and stayed with her family.

Son of the Savannah

The change in fortune of kunsa Badibunka and the fact
that time and distance can make the heart fonder she
started showing signs of breaking down. It is said that one
cannot separate the leopard from it spots nor can we teach
an old dog new tricks.

This applied to Fanta Kurung's friend as she reverted to
the street concealed at first and later doing it openly. Yes,
this village girl, floozy Fanta Kurung's friend, thought her
wiser than all around and that she could place woolen
veils on the faces of the community while doing her dirty
actions.

She got so shameless and nonchalant about her uncouth
behaviors that one day she took all three children of
Kunsa Badibunka with her to her boy friend. When Kunsa
called about it and asked why she associated with such a
friends and did dirty game to him.

She replied by asking if she had no right to get male
friends. That infuriated Kunsa Badibunka but being in
America he had to cool off and sort help by asking friends
and those in the know to look into the story before he
takes drastic action.

Fanta Kurung got worse in the end. She allowed endless
chain of lovers to sleep in while Kunsa's children are
around. Her deranged, if not tangled mind, lead her into
bringing her male partner, monkey face Jeneding Jalong,
to sleep with her while the children were in their rooms.
Lo and behold both she and monkey face miss calculated
the suspicion of the children who pretended to be asleep
when the two arrived at the house. Fanta Kurung even
counter checked to be certain they were asleep.

Not too long the children, while peeping from their door, saw this shameless ad ultra, monkey face, crawl into their mother's room. The children wanted to call the police but could not because they accidentally left their mobiles at their mother's bedroom.

Monkey face had a getaway car parked just two hundred yards from the main gate in the event things went wrong he could escape in seconds from the scenery. Fanta Kurung and monkey face Jeneding Jalong got up 5:30 am and had the nerves to kiss their dirty goodbyes at the center of the yard before full gaze of the children, thinking them asleep. It got so bad that the elder child called Fanta Kurung and placed an ultimatum that next time her lovers sleep in the house she and her sister will run away and never to come back or accept her as their mother.

Fanta kurung grew to be an embarrassment to not only the children but also all kunsa's relatives and friends. In the end none associated with her. She remained aloof as if though in manic denial. Being very comfortable in the villa Kunsa Badibunka built for her in Gambia and him being in America afforded her loose opportunity to regress and revert to her old bad ways i.e. the street, men, and drugs with phi nest.

She stooped so low that adultery became a regular high way for her and her male partner monkey face Jeneding Jalong. This left Kunsa Badibunka depressed for months on end because Fanta Kurung had before their engagement promised never to be a street or 'Gruna-girl' for the rest of her life should he marry her. Concerned friends bombarded Kunsa with sad escapees of Fanta Kurung.

Son of the Savannah

This, Kunsa Badibunka made known to Fatou Kurung but was not tempted to devoice her yet because of his love for her and the children they had in the good days. He never wanted to see his children yarning for a mother or a father. He wants to keep the family unit under one roof and not a separated one where the children will be torn between the parents.

Besides, he loved this lady with every sinew and heart he had and could not recon this beast in a woman's body was what he married. Her acts were so shameful and degrading that he thought a curse must have been cast upon him for leasing his life to such a degrading monster of a prostitute. This once esteemed lady has now turned into an offensive tart and a slut of the highest category and still believes she could fool people into not noticing or seeing through her filthy life.

The threat from the children only made her switch rendezvous zone knowing that the children in a telephone conversation to their dad confirmed their intentions to run away should their mother continue to act so disgracefully and pain it was causing them.

Kunsa Badibunka was so shocked that he called cousin-blest heart Ayata to look into the allegation coming from his children. From that day he channeled the children's allowance through cousin Ayata at the same time he confronted Fatou kurung about the heart wrenching shameless acts. All Fatou Kurung could or was able to say in her defense was she had nothing to say. This alone was a hallmark of guilt. She later threatened the kids to cause the elder one to go to cousin Ayata for few hours to sought solace from the embarrassment.

The straw that almost broke gentle and kind Kunsa Badibunka's back and let pure love sink in the sea of desperation was the deepest and most personal, if not bizarre, experience he and the children ever had to endure. Lasting characteristics makes us who we are and for Fanta Kurung it portrays self-deprecation to say the least.

Nurse Majula, a cousin of Fanta Kurung, tried all she could by counseling and advising the family to take Fanta kurung for expert psychiatric and medical evaluation before things get out of hand further.

Fanta Kurung, in her illusionary, deluded and hallucinatory mine, believes she was maligned by those who wanted money from her. She was just having a good time before her beloved husband returns from America. Her social imbalance seems to be a curse pushing her into earthly hell.

Losing Kunsa Badibunka and the kids would tantamount to irretrievable loss indeed. Some dare think that her current behaviors may be due to cognitive impairment. Kunsa badibunka also held such slim spider's web believe in this likelihood that he vowed not to devoice her while looking for possible cure or psychiatric intervention that could save his lover.

Fanta kurung provided pseudo-psychiatrists a field day of speculations and unfounded conclusions as to why this regression in Fanta Kurung's life. They labeled her current setback as psychotic and hyperactive sex phenomenon. They dared to recommend both cognitive and behavioral therapy in conjunction with local witchcraft approaches.

Son of the Savannah

One beguiles the truth by saying that everything about Fanta Kurung pointed toward a decompensate end-stage of the most romantic affair that ever happened at kandia. Legend has it that Kunsa Badibunka had to come to the Gambia take Fanta Kurung and the children to America where he sought treatment for her.

A miracle never ceases to happen or failed Fanta Kurunga who suddenly recovered and became a shy caring mother. She comfiest of not being aware of the childish and disgraceful acts she was alleged to have been committing. To cut a long story, Kunsa Badibunka being a fighter, completed his law degree at Boston University and established a very big law firm while Fanta Kurung enrolled in computer science course with a major in mathematics at a college nearby.

She graduated magna cum lauded and is now teaching at a junior college with intention of doing a masters degree in science and becoming a professor one fine day. Only pure and unadulterated love glued Kunsa Badibunka to tulunaa Musu, alias Fanta Kurung.

As for her cousins Majula Seyabalo and Kubasa Mori, the call of establishing a medical center to provide medical aid to villagers went exceptionally well. Their center became known worldwide and charitable trusts to help their cause were established in England, America, Spain, and even as far as China and Japan.

Consultants of various specialties in medicine, Obstetrics and Gynecology, Pediatrics, and surgery came from these and far away countries to provide free medical service to the villagers and likewise donated money towards operations of the medical center.

In addition Kunsa Mori became an overnight author of
endless string of books covering many areas of day-to-day
life of the villager, medicine and romantic novels. Fanta
Kurung and kunsa Badibunka were endowed with three
daughters, Famat, Bint, and Yat. Famat, the elder became
a doctor following footsteps of her uncle.

While other two girls, Bint opted for law and Yat became
comfortable with a nursing career. Kunsa Badibunka said
of Fanta Kurung thus that if he had no eyes, his ears
would love her invisible beauty; that if he had no ears, her
outward features would move him.

If neither existed he felt that just touching her would spark
love senses in him. Simply he was blindly in love with
this dame and because of true love he was able to forgive
all her earthly faults. I hope this mirrors our own Alice in
love land experiences or story.

No one is born hating
another person because
of the colour of his skin,
or his background or his
religion. People learn to
hate, and if they can
learn to hate, they can
be taught to love, for
love comes more
naturally to the human
heart than its opposite.

Nelson Mandela

Son of the Savannah
Chapter 8
Life in the USA

Kunsa Badibunka and Fanta Kurung having eventually
patched up their differences and forgave each other
migrated to the United States of America. They started
their new life at Detroit, Michigan, Motor city of
heartland America.

This four million inhabitant city is hub of motor car
industry where big names like Ford, Chrysler, Buick,
general Motors and many other names adorned
signboards. Three quarters of the city are in one form or
the other not only employed by the industry but directly
affiliated too it.

Detroit is one of the most integrated American cities. She
harbors people of all hues from all over the world. Some
of who are students and just fortune seekers. It is home of
Wayne state University and many other excellent learning
and trade institutions.

Detroit is microcosm of America. Kunsa and Fanta rented
a luxurious three bed room flat at Woodward Avenue in
tantalizing Detroit City Michigan. The high street and
skyscrapers are a delight to watch, perambulate or seat at
the entertainment Park.

Soon the couple made friends in the likes of john and
Alison Cruise, Hilda and Homer Sheppard, and many
more than entered. Fanta Kurung attended Detroit College
and studied IT. She graduated Comma magmata at the end
of two years and proceeded to work at General Motors as
IT officer at one of its plants.

As for kunsa Badibunka he did a Master's degree in Biological sciences followed gaining the Doctor of Medicine from the American University of the Caribbean school of Medicine, Plymouth, Montserrat, Wet Indies in 1992.

Dr. Ceesay proudly hugs onto Mother Africa

Dr. Alhasan Sisawo Ceesay, MD

Dr. Kunsa Badibunka, being an ultra nationalist with strong believes that his people back in needed his service far more than super developed America abound with thousands of hospital with modern tools and know compared to impoverish Gambia and deprived rural communities.

It took great convincing effort by Kunsa to get through Fanta's head for she had just started tasting the good life and was not prepared to exchange it with that of mosquito infested and poor sanitation and lack of all amenities she just found possible for humans in the United States. Yes, she finally relented and the couple returned to Gambia in 1992.

Dr. Ceesay and wife Fatou Koma Ceesay, UK 2000

Son of the Savannah

Chapter 9

Manding Medical Centre

Shortly after arrival the couple moved to Panyeki, home of Dr. Kunsa Badibunka. Earlier chapters already gave bird's eye view of Panyeki in Lower Badibou District, the Gambia. When God wants to destroy someone, He first made him an unusual dreamer.

 So Gandhi had his dream of people solving social deference none violently and Rev. Martin Luther king, jr. held onto his admirable dream of children of Jews and Gentile, black and whites holding hands and living in harmony spearheading peaceful cause for mankind. There are the Albert Schweitzer's and mother Theresa's of the world dreamers who spent their lives believing in their dreams for mankind.

My dream, since 1956, was the simple goal of providing medical aid to those far and in remote villages. The villager, who is forced to walk miles on end to seek medical aid for his already dying child, wife or friend, deserves a better health system.

Something I saw in 1956 left an indelible mark in my mind and I have since then asked and prayed that God help me bring part if not full to the kind of tragedy that was passing right before me.

Dr. Alhasan Sisawo Ceesay, MD

I was hopelessly unable to give relief except to comfort those involved. In 1956, while on my way to Saba village, I met an anxious father carrying his son and his almost dead pregnant wife on the back of donkey heading for the health center at Kerewan village, three or more miles from where I met him.

The child was vomiting yellow stuff, he was sweaty, his eyes were reverted backwards and the pregnant lady groaning every time the mule moves. There was some greenish fluid dripping off her lapper. She could barely hold the ropes controlling the donkey.

I went to Kerewan later that evening and asked about the status of that family, only to be told that the boy passed away half a mile to the dispensary and the lady was referred to the central hospital in Banjul but the family had no money to pay for her transportation nor was the River ambulance available as it was undergoing maintenance at the Dockyard.

To cut a long story short, both child and mother died because of lack of medical facilities or modern medical aid to the villager. One or all of those lives could have been saved and remain beneficial to the country than the fate that befell them. I prayed and grieved with the family for months and redoubled my efforts at school in other to solve such development in future.

I committed myself to medicine from that day on and never regretted making such a challenging decision in my life. Hence, when on the day I was taking the Hippocratic Oath, I not only swore to uphold all therein but to make sure that God helped me not to ever deviate from my commitment and promise to be part of the solution in the health services of the Gambia.

I am committed to provide healthcare delivery and education to the villager, and to complement the existing medical facilities in the Gambia as well as ease the shortage of medical service personnel.

 To many, except the dreamer, such path leads to failure as they turn to be white elephants. Some friends tease me by flatly promising to rise from their graves on the opening day of such an Alice in wonderland project.

Let me make it crystal clear that I had no illusions about what was needed, or to be done and that the building of the hospital would indeed be a lifetime challenge I am fully ready to grapple with. There would be a lot of well-wishers but very few will ever want to join until the opening day ceremonies.

Dr. Alhasan Sisawo Ceesay, MD

So first things first, I met an attorney friend Mr. Ousainou Darboe, a villager like me, on September 24, 1992, and pleaded for his assistance with the legal aspects of setting up a charitable foundation, Manding Medical center at Njawara village in the provinces for the sole purpose of providing much needed medical aid to the villager.

He was very obliging and requested no payment in return for his services. In the mean time I got a board of governors elected while he prepared the memorandum and articles of association of Manding Medical Centre at Njawara village.

Also, I met with the Lower Badibou district chief, Kitabou Singateh, who by the way was my primary school class mate at Kinte Kunda from 1953 to 1957, the District Authority, Commissioner and the kerewan Area Council.

All of whom were more than delighted and did all they could under the law to help me set up a grassroots local advisory committee, which was headed by the commissioner, to assist the board and also let the villagers feel being part of the ongoing project.

Son of the Savannah

At my home village, Njawara, a group organized itself and formed a pioneering committee to formally ask the Alkalo (village head/mayor) and the people of Toro Bahen village to donate the earmarked land between it and Njawara for the sole purpose of establishing the Manding Medical Centre on it.

The land issue was partially cleared by the first week of the appeal. In October 1992, Alkalo Omar Koi Bah of Toro Bahen, along with alhaj Musa (Njabi) Bah and Sirimang Bah called my brother, Doudu Ceesay, the elders of Toro Bahen and I to officially inform us that the earmarked land of two plots have been donated to me for the sole purpose of erecting a medical center and hospital facility for the villagers of the region and Gambia. We thanked him for his foresight and kindness towards future generations.

I went back to my lawyer, Ousainu Darboe who by then had finished all work needed for the registration of Manding Medical Centre. We are forever indebted to Alkalos Omar Koi, Arfang Bah, Musa (Njambi) Bah and resident Sirimang Bah, and the people of Toro village. Lastly but not the least our venerable able lawyer Mr. Ousainou Darboe, without whose kindness and legal mind the registration of Manding Medical Centre would have taken longer that it did assisted me.

I also express profound gratitude to the Hon. Chief of Lower Badibou district, Kitabou Singateh, the commissioner, and the local district authority for their understanding and willingness to contribute positively towards our goal and growth.

I submitted the registration application material to the Attorney General's Chambers at the Justice Department, Banjul, on October 22, 1992 and Manding Medical Centre was officially registered as an incorporated charitable organization under the companies Act, 1959 by the 27th of October 1992. Manding Medical Centre' certificate of incorporation is number: 224/1992.

With the completion of the paper work and registration of the centre, I embarked on a blitz of letter writing informing philanthropists and organizations worldwide about Manding Medical Centre and the need for assistance or donations of medications, equipments, medical videos with which to teach our cadre and villagers to become health worker or evangelist, or nurses and to help us build the centre. To complete the establishment process, after the land was officially ours, I wrote to the following letter to the Ministry of Health informing them of the formation of Manding Medical Centre, a self –help health organization at Njawara, Lower Badibou, NBD, the Gambia.

Son of the Savannah

Our temporal address was at 5B Ingram Street in Banjul, capital of the Gambia.

Manding Medical Centre

5B Ingram Street

Banjul, The Gambia

March 2, 1993

Permanent Secretary

Ministry of Health

The Quadrangle

Banjul, The Gambia

West Africa

Dear Permanent Secretary

Re: Application for the establishment of a Medical Centre at Njawara in the North Bank.

We are pleased to bring to attention the setting up of a self-help Health organization in the North Bank Division at Njawara village.

Dr. Alhasan Sisawo Ceesay, MD

The directorates and members of the organization would be more than grateful if the Ministry of Health would allow us establish Manding Medical Centre at Njawara village, Lower Badibou District of the Gambia. Manding Medical Centre, when fully operational, will provide medical, surgical, gynecological and obstetrics, Pediatrics and other facilities to the villagers.

It will also help ease the shortage of medical facilities in that region. Manding Medical Centre will have health education secessions in the villages as an effort to enlighten our youths.

Again, thank you for taking time to consider our application and we certainly look forward to a positive recognition of the need for such a centre in the rural sector of the Gambia.

I am anxiously waiting to hear from your office at your convenience. Regards

Yours sincerely

Dr. Alhasan S. Ceesay, MD

Director/Coordinator

Meanwhile the villagers grew more enthused and throngs of them attended our monthly health field trips or clinics.

The attendance grew so large that we ended up listing the villages to attend in turn of nine villages per trip. This usually totals to a bit above 1,000 patients at a given visit. I normally go on weekends with three doctors and at times four volunteer doctors along with Nurses aid Mrs.

Mbee Sonko and Ida Njie to assist us do the job. The field trips/clinics start with an announcement by Radio Gambia giving the names of villages expected to attend and at which village health centre. The clinic day starts with an early morning breakfast by the team and then a ride to the village health centre where we would find the villagers and their sick ones assembled.

Every occasion starts with the offering of prayers and then the various village heads, in attendance help us in organizing the flow of people wanting to be see by one of our team doctors. In most cases the day goes trouble free but at certain localities the political tension does make it very difficult to have such large groups of people without little arguments.

Thanks to the Commissioner (s) for deploying the police or making them available to quell trouble and help us maintain order during these clinics. Commissioner Lamin Koma can tell you how rough things can be at some of these clinic centres.

Dr. Alhasan Sisawo Ceesay, MD

He was trapped in one of these bad moments of people rushing to be in the front line of the queue to see one our doctors. The Ministry of Health finally sent us the following affirmative reply as thus: -

Ministry of Health & Social services

The Quadrangle

Banjul, The Gambia

Ref.P510/289/01(95)

Dr. Alhasan Ceesay

Manding Medical Centre

5B Ingram Street

Banjul, The Gambia

RE: Application to establish a Medical Centre at Njawara

I acknowledge receipt of your letter of the 2nd March 1993 on the above-mentioned subject. I wish to inform you that this Ministry has no objection to your application to establish Manding Medical Centre at Njawara.

This initiative is in line with our national health policies and we would render our support in our joint efforts to improve the health of the people.

Signed: N. Ceesay

For Permanent Secretary

After several more field trips it was suggested we apply for a None Governmental Organization (NGO) status. It was believed that if we become and NGO, help would come our way quicker.

I went to work on this suggestion and arranged for Tango Secretariat Centre to send one of the United Nations voluntary program officers to come and evaluate our performance relative to the objectives of Manding Medical Centre.

This was accepted and a field trip was set up for September 12 to 22, 1995. Radio Gambia made the announcement well ahead of the time for our arrival and the following was the outcome of that august gathering of September 21 &22, 1995.

Dr. Alhasan Sisawo Ceesay, MD

Dr. Alhasan S. Ceesay, MD

Njawara School in seccession 2005

Chapter 10

TANGO SECRETARIAT TRIP REPORT ON MANDING MEDICAL CENTRE, SEPTEMBER 21 – 22, 1995

A field trip to Kerewan at the North Bank Division was organized by the Manding Medical Centre Executive Director Dr. Alhasan S. Ceesay in conjunction with Tango Secretariat Centre to see the organization's activities and meet the members before recommending the organization as a member of Tango.

On September 21, 1995, two meetings were organized in two big centers where members gather to air their views and experience from the organization. Alkalos, chiefs, imams, women, men and youths attended these meetings. The key leadership from five villages in their speeches showed interest and support for the project and organization.

Alkalo of Toro Bahen Omar Koi and chiefs donated the land for the constructing of Manding Medical Centre, the hospital and its ancillaries. The two meeting were highly attended and successful.

Dr. Alhasan Sisawo Ceesay, MD

The Tango (UNV) program officer Mr. Muloshi on behalf of Tango gave a keynote speech on Tango's operations and activities as an umbrella organization and urged members to work hand in hand with the organization in their efforts to develop their villages and North Bank area.

The three meetings with the commissioner during the field trip on our courtesy call were successful and encouraged the executive Director of Manding Medical Centre, Dr. Alhasan Ceesay, to cooperate with the strict, especially the commissioner who is one of the advisors in the local committee.

The commissioner thanked Tango for making the purpose of the mission clear to him and promised that he will try by all means to cooperate with Tango in the area of Technical advice and institution capacity building. Clinic day was organized on September 22, 1995 at Njawara and 150 people attended and got treatments.

RECOMMENDATION

Looking at the caliber of leadership and development activities compared to some NGO tango members in comparison to Manding Medical Centre, the organization need consideration since they have already activities with a promising future.

Looking at the composition of the Board, they have people with a great vision. They have strong membership and backup at the grassroots levels. The organization has chosen to do what is right at the right time and their concentration in one area is vital and a good starting point.

Any success achieved by any organization depended on good leadership and discipline. Manding Medical Centre has quality leadership and deserves NGO status.

Signed: M. Muloshi

UNV Program Officer

We were delighted by the recommendation made by the United Nations voluntary Program Officer in the Gambia. We redoubled our efforts to contact organizations seeking help worldwide.

In between letters and monthly field trips to different select health centres we were blessed with visits from interested friends and groups or representatives of similar organizations in the globe. I had several telephone calls to Dr. Edward Brown, an official of the World Bank in Washington, D. C. responsible of the bank's health affairs at the time.

Dr. Alhasan Sisawo Ceesay, MD

He was very receptive and had several added discussions with Dentist Melvin George, then Director of Medical and Health Service for the Gambia, on how the bank could help in the financing of the building of Manding Medical Centre.

These talks went on well and Dr. Edward brown gave me his promise and personal commitment to helping the project and that we have to start in a small scale and the building will have to be done in several well planned phases. Dr. Sidi C. Jammeh, a former Armitage School colleague, promised to help me by constantly reminding Dr. Brown of the need to help us with the project.

This kept the momentum at the World Bank alive for Manding Medical Centre. Among our guest were a couple from Colchester, Essex, UK, Lorna V. Robinson and husband Keith Robinson were very impressed by our project and enthusiasm of the ordinary villagers about Manding Medical Centre.

They fell in love with the idea and objectives of the self-help health organization and promised to help as much as they could. We had by this time submitted application for NGO status and ACCNO Secretary replied thus:

Son of the savannah

ACCNO Secretariat

Dept. of Community Development

13 Mariner Parade

Babjul, The Gambia

September 12, 1994

Ref.CD/ACCNO/Vol3/(183)

Dr. Alhasan S. Ceesay

Director/Coordinator

Manding Medical Centre

P. O. Box 640

Banjul, The Gambia

Dear Sir,

RE: application for an NGO status within the ACCNO framework

Dr. Alhasan Sisawo Ceesay, MD

Please find enclosed a self-explanatory letter from the Ministry for local government and lands concerning the approval of your application for NGO status. ACCCNO Secretariat congratulates your organization for successfully completing the registration process and wishes you a fruitful relationship in the field of development.

Thank you for your cooperation

Yours Faithfully

Musu Ngujo

For: ACCNO desk Officer

Cc: file & R/File

Replies from our worldwide appeal letters did not pour in money nor did these materialized beyond promises to help in due course.

Hence, I decided to open up a pharmacy at my expense at my residence in the Bundung area of Serekunda using the proceeds from its sales to finance the health field trips and activities of the organization.

This meant spending an extra three to four hours at the pharmacy daily after eight hours at the RVH before rejoining my family.

All drugs used for the treatment of patients at our field trip clinics were purchased from sales I made at the Bundung Pharmacy. A local agency, known as IBAS, lent me D8000, interest free, which was used in buying drugs and paying for transportation for the project's activities. The loan was completely repaid well ahead of the allowed sixteen months period given by IBAS.

We are obliged and grateful to Aja Ndey Oley Jobe and management of IBAS for their kindness to assist us at the time. Just when things were about to be financially complete for us to start the first phase of building the various sections of the hospital, came the unexpected coup d'etat of July 22, 1994.

The reaction from would be our donors and supporters or sponsors were swift and equally unexpected. All those who were considering giving the project a chance sited likelihood of sudden national unrest and instability as reasons for their withdrawal of promised aid and participation while some suggested my waiting until after the transition phase of the coup d'etat before they would reconsider reopening our files with them.

Again it resorted to legend or case of the chicken the egg, which came first as no one, knew when the transition would end and we kept our fingers crossed hoping that daylight will be ours in not far distance.

It was a severe blow to our hope and for getting the type of interest and support that was engendered for Manding Medical Centre would be difficult to match after such crisis that occurred in the Gambia.

Many were acting in conjunction with their governments, which were not sure of what the future under military rule would be for the Gambia. All prospective and possible international sources earmarked for Manding Medical Centre were either frozen or evaporated into thin air with the coup leaving me floating in the middle of the ocean of despair without a life jacket except God's merciful hands.

I knew the villagers would grow restless if nothing happens in the direction of building the centre. I called an emergency general meeting with members from most of the villages and told them of the new challenge and development and this information not only fell on deaf ears but left their spirits dampened.

Interest waxed and waned at some quarters but I kept on trying my best not to be despondent like the others have shown. I kept the organization alive under very limited funds raised from the pharmacy at Bundung until my trip to the UK in January 2000.

Before leaving the Gambia, the Commissioner for north Bank Division and chairman of the local advisory committee for Manding Medical Centre, Mr. Lamin Koma, gave me the following letter to assist me in my fund raising drive while in England and possible other European countries. It read thus:

The Commissioner

Kerewan Village

North Bank Division

The Gambia, West Africa

June 15, 1998

TO WHOM IT MAY CONCERN

I hereby write to testify and confirm that Manding Medical Centre is a self-help health project situated at Njawara village, North Bank Division.

Dr. Alhasan Sisawo Ceesay, MD

As the Commissioner of this division I was elected as the Chairman of the local advisory Committee of the Manding Medical Centre. As I am concerned, I am aware of this self-help project since it took off the ground, by the able hands of Dr. Alhasan S. Ceesay, a born citizen of Njawara village.

The purpose of the establishing of such a medical centre is to provide medical attention/care to all Gambians irrespective of religion, tribe, nationality or gender and age within the country and sub-region.

It is in these regards that this office writes to seek for your assistance in providing support in cash/kind to make this medical center a reality. I look forward to your continued support and cooperation.

Signed: V. Baldeh

For Commissioner

North Bank Division

The new millennium started with good omen for Manding Medical Centre. I have been invited to go to Europe and America on a fund raising trip for the centre but could not because of my commitment with the Royal Victoria Hospital (RVH).

The best time would be during the vacation period to be able to travel and keep my job at the same time.

Above all my family needed the monetary support, which would fade away if I lost the post at the RVH.

Hence, to my delight and greatest timely occurrence I heard from my long-standing friend in Colchester, Mrs. Lorna V. Robinson, inviting my wife and I to come to the UK to attend the wedding of their younger daughter on January 9th, 2000. Coincidentally, I had just started my annual leave, which was to finish on the 26th of January 2000.

The excitement mounted when we received a fax from the visa officer at the British High Commission in the Gambia requesting that we report to the visa processing office with our passports on Tuesday 8.30 am January 4th, 2000 for processing of our visas for our pending travels to the UK.

This took me by surprise because of the casual way we had discussed the possibility of such a trip. So when we got the telephone call followed by the said fax from the visa section I was caught off guard and had to rush through all the preparations for my wife and I to travel to UK without a second thought on whether adequate arrangements were being made for my eventual pursuit of a postgraduate degree (MRCP) in internal medicine.

Hind side has it that I needed to discuss this aspect with the visa counsellor and request for eventual student visa status or leave to remain until my completion of the post graduate degree I wanted to pursue.

Miss Famatanding Ceesay, Daughter

Son of the Savannah

God's ways and timing are best for every occasion. I was yearning to get a way out of the financial limbo the center ran into since the change of government in the Gambia. Now that opportunity was suddenly thrown on my laps by Lorna Robinson's open-ended invitation for my wife and to attend their daughter's wedding ceremony in the UK.

Interested donors started being weary about Military rule and possible restlessness that may ensue. Hence, Manding Medical Centre literally lost all its prospective overseas support as well as sponsors most of who had cold feet after the July coup d'etat of 2004.

I ended up running the centre from my meager salary of D1500 or seventy-five pounds sterling per month and of literally hard labor with long hours at a time. The other source was from what little I could make from sales at the Bundung pharmacy.

To cut a long story short we were granted visas to travel to the UK. We left the Gambia on the 6th of January 2000 on a new footing and challenge to bring back some life into Manding Medical centre while in England. I got on the ball as soon as the wedding ceremony was over. I obtained a three–year study leave from the Management Board of the Royal Victoria Hospital in Banjul.

This gave me all the time I needed to try to rekindle interest in the center and thereby inject into Manding Medical center cash flow it needed to help us meet or our targeted goal and objective for the farming community in the North Bank Division of the Gambia. It was more like a miracle entering this new concrete and direct ways.

Help from my host Lorna Robinson of Colchester, Essex, UK further anointed my hands. Lorna and I wrote several letters to various places, including celebrities and organizations, most of who replied in the negative because of perception they had about the political climate in Gambia since the coup d'etat of July 22nd 1994.

Nonetheless some hinted being interested at a later date, meaning when the solders return to camp. A few donated small amounts plus hospital items. By now it became clear that we have to counter the perception most, on this side of the isles feel or had about the Gambia at the time.

This dreadful start did not alarm me much for I am fully aware of the wrong information about the average African in the village, who like most, is just a decent human being trying to earn an honest living for himself, family and community.

Villagers are least interested in all the political gimmickry shrouding and clothing their lives. I do not at all blame the rest of world for getting sick and tired of helping and not seeing any tangible good come out of it and worse some African politicians and regimes show no interest in helping move the African people onto better and modern rewarding modalities of life.

They offer more lip service than opening avenues for progress. How many knew that the Ethiopian starvation was politically orchestrated by the then Mangestu regime? Genocide regime and the heartlessness of some African politicians made me feel sick.

To remove any possible sceptics regarding Manding Medical Centre and its objectives we decided to have it registered as a charitable organization in the UK under the name of Colchester Friends of Manding charitable trust. The Robinson knew a solicitor who would be so kind to help us with the legal aspect of the registration process with UK charity Commission.

They spoke to Mr. Bruce Ballard of the Birkett long Solicitors to come to our aid. This kind gentleman, like my lawyer friend, Mr. Ousainou Darboe, gladly agreed to help and sent us a draft of the Trust deed.

Dr. Alhasan Sisawo Ceesay, MD

After a series of changes were made on the draft he forwarded our request to be registered in the UK as a charitable organization helping its twin partner or parent group, Manding Medical Centre at Njawara village in the Gambia, West Africa.

Meanwhile, we concentrated our activities through media campaign effort to call attention to existence of Friends of Manding and their desire in building a hospital for Manding Medical Centre at Njawara, the Gambia. Again we ran into a very gentle heart in the person of Miss Helen Anderson of Colchester who was the Community website editor for Essex County.

She went head over heels regarding the idea of helping others so far away when approached by Lorna Robinson. Helen thought the idea wonderful and at the same time helped us have our own website and also had an article published by the Evening Gazette which had a large reader circulation.

In the same vein I got the interest of Dr. Linda Mahon-Daly, Dr. Peter Wilson, Dr. Laurel Spooner, Dr. Richard Spooner, Dr. Philip Murray, Dr. Barbara Murray, Dr. Fredric Payne, who by the way was our Medical superintendent under who I worked at the RVH during the later part of colonial Gambia, along with many surgeries in the Colchester area.

Son the Savannah

These were my Good Samaritans of the day who worked acidulously to make Manding Medical Centre become a reality for the villagers in the Gambia. Dr. Linda Mahon-Daly helped distribute letters about Manding Medical Centre to nearly all her colleagues in the Colchester Borough and so did Dr. Laurel Spooner.

Bless their hearts for kindness and job well done. The news article published by the Evening Gazette brought us another very helpful and kind person, Mr. Malkait singh who is an ophthalmologist and had made several trips to the Gambia before knowing about the Friends of Manding.

He was delighted to join Neville Thompson, Connie Thompson, Lorna Robinson, Keith Robinson, Loenard Thompson, Mark Naylor, Barbara Philips and others as pioneering members of Friends of Manding. Mr. Malkait Singh and I grew to be very good friends and he had since given me lots of personal monetary help to cater for my exams and family back in the Gambia.

I am very grateful for interest and kindness, and concern he showed about my family. A few months after the formation of Friends of Manding, Dr. Laurel Spooner spent a week in the Gambia vacationing and doing some fact finding about the centre.

Dr. Alhasan Sisawo Ceesay, MD

During which time she visited Manding Medical Centre at Njawara in the North Bank Division. The villagers were happy to meet her and thanked her about good work being done in Colchester regarding Manding Medical Centre.

Everyone was happy about the news that people in the UK were poised to assist Manding Medical Centre goes forward in its drive to provide medical aid to villagers. A meeting of member of the Friends of Manding was scheduled for the first week of February 2001.

Mean while our solicitor continued pressing for registration of Friends of Manding, which is the arm and Manding Medical Centre's Colchester branch support group, as charity in the UK.

Dr. Laurel Spooner suggested we start with small-scale form of the centre and then gradually expand as funds become available. This consideration would be studied in full and deliberated upon by the committee during the forth-coming February meeting.

Keith, Dr. Ceesay, and Mrs. Lorna Robinson

Dr. Alhasan Sisawo Ceesay, MD

Miss Binta Ceesay, Daughter

Chapter 11

WHAT IS MANDING MEDICAL CENTRE?

Manding Medical Centre, located at Njawara village in the North Bank Region, Gambia, West Africa, is a self-help village health organization founded by Dr. Alhasan S. Ceesay. Its objective is to provide medical service to the villagers by providing efficient and affordable medical aid to all people in and around the Gambia, especially the rural sector.

We are dedicated to relieving suffering and ensure effective treatment for villagers and all attending Manding Medical Centre at Njawara, NBR.

ESTABLISHED

The Manding Medical Centre is founded by Dr. Alhasan Sisawo Ceesay, a native of Njawara village in 1992, because of sheer shortage of medical service to the region and the preponderance of premature deaths by children from Malaria, malnutrition, diarrhea, and worm infestations. These childhood maladies account for almost 25% of Gambian children's death before the age of five years.

Dr. Algasan Sisawo Ceesay, MD

The Gambia Ministry of Health officially recognized the Centre in 1995 and prior to which it became a None Governmental Organization (NGO) on September 12th, 1994. In addition, the Manding Medical Centre now has Friends of Manding Charitable Trust, Colchester, Essex, UK as its arm and liaison in the UK and the European Union countries.

The Friends of Manding is a registered charity in England and Wales. Its registration number is 1088136 since August 21, 2001. In similar development and purpose, Dr. Avery Aten heads the Friends of Manding Alpena Charitable Trust, Alpena, Michigan, UAS since May 2005.

MISSION STATEMENT

Suffering in another human being is a call to the rest of us to stand in fellowship. It requires us to be there and it is a mystery, which demands the spirit of caring, sharing and our presence. Our duty as healthcare professionals is providing medical care, which is a fundamental right of all human beings.

This village health organization is dedicated to providing medical aid to the rural sector and farming community in the Gambia. It will compliment the health service in the Gambia in addition it will promote preventive medicine in the hinterland of the Gambia.

MEMBERSHIP

Well over twenty thousand villagers, comprising of farmers, village heads, and chiefs, the Kerewan Area Council, Commissioners and local District Authority are now fully active enthusiastic members of Manding Medical Centre.

All are welcomed to join the endeavors of the center. People from the rest of the globe are more than welcomed to participate or share with us our dream in bring much needed medical service to people in desperate state because of lack of medical facilities.

ACTIVITIES

Manding Medical Centre tries to alleviate some of the above mentioned health problems and situations by having bimonthly health field trips/clinics to villages teaching them about health, preventive medicine and hygiene that would help reduce the number infected and the vectors responsible for these diseases.

We encourage antenatal and postnatal attendance of clinics by mothers and we treat the sick amongst them with minimum charge to not so elderly and pregnant young ladies.

Dr. Alhasan Sisawo Ceesay, MD

The service is free to children, the very elderly, and the indigent needing emergency treatment. The rest pay amounts well below tat in private practice. Money accrued is subsequently used to buy drugs with which to treat the patients and for other projects of the centre. When in cession the centre treats well more than 1000 patients per field trip to the villages.

We provide free information and advisory service on aids and sexually transmitted diseases (STDs) to the young, all patients, their relatives and friends. We also plan to have a Nursing School in due course to augment not only staff but also the government health centres when the need arises.

IMMEDIATE GOAL AND APPEAL

The villagers are very enthused about the center and Toro Bahen village, next to Njawara village, has donated two plots of land for the building of the centre and its ancillary units, which is now leased to Manding medical centre for ninety-nine years. More than 2000 children die tragically from malaria and other childhood ailments stated above for shortage of health services.

We are eager to start building the children' and maternity wings of the proposed Gambia General Hospital at Manding Medical Centre and do need raise the required 900,000 pounds sterling to accomplish our goal.

Ten bags of cement cost thirty pounds sterling or $60 (sixty us dollars). Also we would be most grateful if we could be assisted with medicines and equipment to facilitate our work. Hence we implore you to kindly support our yearning to build the children' and maternity wings of Manding Medical Centre.

We are dedicated to providing medical aid to the villager, especially children. We are investors in people and you are invited to join the endeavors of Manding Medical Centre at Njawara village, the Gambia, West Africa. Help us make a difference and beacon of hope for the villagers. Please give generously.

Today's hope can be tomorrow's reality. We want to contribute positively towards the health services of the Gambia, and with this center in place it will create greater health awareness and privation by the villagers.

Cash contributions of any amount should be sent in the name of Manding Medical Centre, to the Friends of Manding charitable Trust, 82 Finchingfield Way, Blackheath, Colchester, Essex, CO2 OAU, and England.

Dr. Alhasan Sisawo Ceesay, MD

It is vital to be certain that Dr. Alhasan S. Ceesay is informed of your contribution via email thus: alhasanceesay@hotmail.co.uk. Your kindness and humane consideration to help save lives will always be deeply appreciated and grateful for by the villagers, the Gambia and I.

OVERSEASES LINKS

The Friends of Manding in Colchester, Essex County, UK, is formed by a local group of residents, doctors, and nurses who regularly visited the Gambia and is in support of Manding Medical Centre. Manding medical center through the auspices of the Friends of Manding recently received recognition and registration by the UK Charity Commission.

They serve as support and our liaison in the Europe Union. The Friends of Manding in behalf of Manding Medical Centre at Njawara has been entered in the central Register of charities with effect from August 21, 2001; the registration number is 1088136 for England and Wales.

Also, a similar charitable trust, the Alpena Friends of Manding Charitable Trust of Michigan, USA, has been established in Alpena, Michigan in June 2006.

It's headed by Dr. Avery Aten a resident physician chairman of the Women and newborn of the Alpena region Community Health along with the medical community of Alpena.

Ntoro Bahen village, Badibou, NBR, The Gambia

Dr. Alhasan Sisawi Ceesay, MD

Chapter 12

MANDING MEDICAL CENTRE MILESTONES

Manding Medical Centre has been in my mind's drawing board since the early 1950s but it took off in earnest when I returned to the Gambia, after graduating from medical school in 1992. The Centre is registered as a charity with the Attorney general's Office, Department of Justice, Banjul, The Gambia, since 1993.

The Gambia Ministry of Health also recognized it in the same year. Toro Bahen village, Lower Badibou, NBD, Gambia, donated two huge plots of land for the location of the center in 1993.

Our none governmental (NGO) status was approved in 1994. On September 21, 1995 Tango Secretariat sent a United Nations voluntary program Officer, Mr. Muloshi on field trip to evaluate the organizational and extent of support for Manding Medical Centre at Njawara village.

Mr. Muloshi's recommendation after two days field trip to the region stated thus; "Looking at the calibre of leadership and development activities to some NGO Tango members in comparison to Manding Medical Centre, the organization need consideration since they have already activities with a promising future.

Looking at composition of the Board, they have people with a vision. They have strong membership and backup at grass root levels. The organization has chosen to what is right at the right time and their concentration in one area is vital and good starting point.

Any success achieved by any group or organization depends on good leadership and discipline. Manding Medical Centre has high quality leadership and deserves NGO status." It was not until my travels to the UK in 2000 that the Friends of Manding Charitable Trust was formed and registered as charity in England and Wales by the UK Charity Commission.

Friends of Manding is the extended arm of Manding Medical Centre at Njawara, The Gambia. They serve as our liaison in the UK and the European Union. Please browse on our website thus: http://friendsofmandinggambimed.btck.co.uk, to learn more or for further information about our work and organization.

We are still on fund raising activities to earn enough to enable us build the children' and maternity units of the hospital at Manding Medical Centre at Njawara. In May 2005, 11 American students and their instructor Mr. Thomas Ray visited Manding Medical Centre at Njawara.

Dr. Alhasan Sisawo Ceesay, MD

Additionally, input from has now resulted in Alpena City, Michigan, USA, twining by proclamation with Njawara and Kinte kunda villages in Gambia respectively on the 5th of December 2005.

In June 2006, Dr. Avery Aten, Chairman of the Women and Newborn of Alpena Region Health Community along with the medical community of Alpena commenced processing application for a charitable Trust to be named Alpena friends of Manding Charitable Trust, Michigan, USA.

This will soon be finalized and up and running to help Dr. Alhasan Ceesay in the provision of medicine and educational assistance to schools in the Lower Badibou district, the Gambia, West Africa.

In August 2008, Dr. Alhasan Ceesay and the Badibou Cultural Dance Troupe will visit Alpena and other cities in Michigan for fund raising drive to enable the building of the Manding Medical Centre children and maternity units at Njawara village.

Dr. Richard Bates, an Obyng, and a number of medical professionals involved in obstetrics and gynecology at Alpena, Michigan joined Manding Medical Centre's crusade on 17/08/07.

Chapter 13

TEMPLATE FOR REGIONAL DEVELOPMENT

Manding Medical Centre became a template for districts elsewhere and villagers to nurture, develop further and handover to the next generation. This None Governmental Health Organization epitomizes a developmental watchtower for the region.

Manding medical center is a pulsating source of hope, jobs training and superb medical service at Njawara village the Gambia. Everyone knows that government alone does not move things fast enough. Society must be radical and pragmatic to pitch into its development.

We know all too well that the developed world got where it is because private efforts were self prophetic and projects like Manding Medical Centre goes long ways to initiate and stimulate community to work together for a positive agenda for its people.

Hence after many years of foot dragging and vicissitude by society I decided I will build the hospital if I have to single-handed. I worked years receiving no government assistance and without grants from the great of the Gambian community.

Dr. Alhasan Sisawo Ceesay, MD

Manding Medical Centre is a positive good that help our regions to cross the road to a better healthcare delivery. We thank everyone for making it possible that our center became a platform and guide in rejuvenating our regions.

We now provide medical service to all Gambians and none Gambians domiciled in the Gambia. We will create more jobs as need arises. This was the reason why I gave my life's comfort for reward that will benefit most needy villagers. It came through determination and kindness of many people worldwide.

There are some things only governments can do but together communities through collective initiatives can achieve at least fifty percent of their developmental needs in addition to government effort.

Today some see Manding medical centre as perpetual monument of good, an honour to the country and a general benefit to villagers and children in the North Bank of the Gambia. Manding medical centre is an inspiration and cause for thankfulness and celebration.

Miss Roheyata Ceesay, Daughter

Dr. Alhasan Sisawo Ceesay, MD

Chapter 14

AN APPEAL TO INTERNATIONAL COMMUNITY

Dear Readers,

The above information about Manding Medical Centre is included in this work only hoping that it will help spread the word more extensively and draw awareness to a greater community of people and readers of my work.

It's my belief that lots of good people out there may want to participate or give to the cause and goal of the centre should they be aware of its existents for the villagers. Hence, I am appealing for help and participatory support from all able to extend their hearts to make this much needed medical endeavour to come to fruition for the rural sector of the Gambia.

Who knows you might even end up coming to bask in our beautiful seaside and relish Gambian generosity. Music for me is reaching out to help others and my patients are yearning for your kind participation and donation in cash/kind. Thanks a million for considering our appeal. God blesses your heart(s). I write with believe that by it money can be generated to provide a much needed medical service to the rural sector. Writing about the Manding Medical Centre may course some Good Samaritan and any wanting to leave foot prints on the sand of time for a good cause to come to our assistance to help us meet the goals of the centre at Njawara village, the Gambia, West Africa. My head, heart and soul are devoted to my family, the Gambia and Manding Medical Centre. It is not a God given calling but a mere conviction that our rural folks deserve better health service than currently available and hence human calling to want to contribute positively to bring resolution of some of our rural health service inadequacies.

I never had an angel come down to me nor have I ever heard the voices of God saying, "Ceesay, you must do so and so" as many mocked Manding Medical Centre emanated from sheer conviction that it is a dutiful way of doing the right thing for curbing premature deaths of children before reaching 5 years of life from malaria, water born diseases, and warm infestations; and in the same vein providing both pre and postnatal care to the pregnant. Hence, portions of proceeds of sales in all my work go to help meet the centre's operational costs and in providing scholarship to indigent indigenous rural candidates due course return to serve rural Gambia wishing to read for a medical degree or agriculture and Medicine. Signed: Dr. Alhasan S. Ceesay, MD/Email: alhasanceesay@hotmail.com

Dr. Alhasan Sisawo Ceesay, MD

Chapter 15

LORNA ROBINSON, AN ANGEL OF MERCY

Keith, Dr. Ceesay, & late Lorna Robinson

Son of the Savannah

There are certain moulds God broke them moments after He finished making them. Mrs. Lorna V. Robinson was one of these unique, caring, sharing and rare angels of mercy. Mrs. Lorna Robinson and I met through her job as general nurse at the then Essex County General hospital in Colchester, Essex County in 1990, when I was a trainee doctor at the hospital.

She and husband Keith Robinson became my friends as far back as in the 1990s and one of their annual pilgrimages is visiting my family in the Gambia, West Africa. This benevolent couple has since been my Colchester if not my England.

Together we set to catch a dream of providing medical aid and service to Gambian villagers. I left at the end of my training to serve my country in 1992. In December 1999 Mrs. Lorna Robinson sent an invitation for my wife and I to attend wedding of Miss Fiona Robinson, her younger daughter, to gentleman Reeves.

We have since 2000 worked acidulously to make the above goal come to fruition, especially for those in the rural sector of the North Bank Region of the Gambia. It was Lorna's joint effort with, nurses, Doctors Laurel Spooner, Barbara Murray, Richard Spooner, Phil Murray, Linda Mahon-Daly, Peter R. Wilson, Malkait Singh and residents of Colchester, which lead to the formation of the Colchester Friends of Manding Charitable Trust. It was registered as a charity in England and Wales in 2001. The charity number is 1088136. This charity acts as liaison in the European Union countries for Manding Medical Centre at Njawara village in the Badibous of the North Bank Region, the Gambia.

Since its conception, the Friends of Manding Charitable Trust had busied itself on weekly or bimonthly Gambi-barzaars in an effort to help raise money for building of both the children and maternity units of the center.

Mrs. Lorna Robinson spent countless week-ends either selling material such as toys, coats and anything she could lay her hands on as long as she believes it will generate money for the building of the children and maternity units of the center.

She spent most of her retirement time organizing activity for the center to help promote our cause. She sent books, spectacles, pens and pencils along with medication for the center's use.

The influence of this Good Samaritan group in Colchester reverberated and lead to the formation of a similar charity group in America, which is lead by Dr. Avery Aten, Alpena Friends of Manding Charitable Trust, Michigan, USA, was formed in May 2005.

Son of the Savannah

All this came about because Mrs. Lorna V. Robinson, the lady of mercy behind the wheel, would not rest while the indigent goes without the most basic things in life. Here is how Lorna views her part during one of many conversations we had about the need to share worth and ourselves with other less fortunate than us.

She simply said, "Ceesay, I feel delighted and warm at heart in helping others, like the villagers. I strongly belief good used could be made from my work and experience I had at the NHS over years.

I will try to recruit as many retired nurses to our cadre as long as they listen to my please. The other secrete is that such activity keeps me young, participating and contributing to the needy. I feel alive and forever growing. In life we most extend our hearts to others and with compassion reach the needy."

This tit bit tells about the unselfish nature of Mrs. Lorna V. Robinson who through the years since her retirement gave her all to help others, especially the villagers, breath a sigh of relief and to have hope and knowledge that someone far away they never met cared about them. Lorna continued saying, "It brings joy to my heart when I share the little I have with the needy. It helps to uplift the despondent.

Dr. Alhasan Sisawo Ceesay, MD

Millions suffer needlessly for not having means of proper health care, clean and safe water, good shelter and chance to attend schools. I want to help you get the villagers from a downward spiral of deepening health deprivation.

I certainly take hope in people like you and your stand to help your folks back home in the Gambia." It was this unique caring angel that I lost on the third of March 2010 for she returned peacefully to her maker on this day. The above was my Lorna and now I cry, when shall we be blessed will another like her?

Losing Lorna Robinson left me feeling that I lost the best person, outside of my family, I ever known. She was a kind soul of unswerving determination to share the little She had with the little guy needing her help. She stood by my cause in thick and thin moments of my stay in the United Kingdom.

Dr. Alhasan S. Ceesay graduating from the American
University of the Caribbean, West Indies, 1992

Dr. Alhasan Sisawo Ceesay, MD

The provision of medical care to villagers is more than a responsibility; it is a sacred trust for me. I will not the villagers or memory Mrs. Lorna V. Robinson down because I believe in looking to the well being of the less fortunate. One carries on trying on reflecting on all the children and villagers who need this health care. Hence no trepidation will hold me back.

My family, the villagers and I miss and deeply mourn her premature departure from mother earth. May she rest in peace with her maker and may we the living without fail or fear able to follow the high shining examples of indefatigable Good Samaritan she was in life.

I hope you will join me to keep her memory and legacy alive for other to copy while we continue taking medical aid to villagers in rural Gambia. Lorna V. Robinson thanks a million and goodbye for now.

Signed: Dr. Alhasan S. Ceesay, MD

Manding Medical Centre, Njawara

The Gambia, West Africa. E-mail: alhasanceesay@hotmail.com

Chapter 16

MY SAMARITAN MEN OF GOOD WILL

Every successful person had Samaritan angels who Offered their shoulders for him or her to stand on and see further than most. Compiled herein are my Samaritan men of goodwill. Hence, I beg leave to indulge in a bit of sentimentality about a few rare human angels who played major part in today's success and help for my villagers.

Believe me their moulds, as you will soon find, are beyond those of simple people. These men help me reach today's pedestal. In medicine for the villager, I profiled ladies who championed my cause. Now, bear with me for just a few lines on the Samaritan men of goodwill.

They like the previously mentioned ladies al not only believe in my dream and objective for the villager but also gave all they could to help make that dream come to fruition.

These men gave unparalleled needed help and friendship to me when I was distressed and in utter despair and darkness. Some even shed a few tears with me because the pain and set back certain roadblocks caused my goal.

Son of the Savannah

One of these was the day I received GMC' e-mail of the 17th June 2008 recanting recognition of my primary medical qualification based on frivolous website enter. Hell brewed to its hottest temperatures, as it took time to unravel the misunderstanding, before GMC rectified the error.

However, with your indulgence let us start from the beginning of the geneses. It was with God' anointing hand in conjunction with Sisawo Bajo Ceesay, alias Sisawo Sallah) that my twin partner I landed on this Garden of Eden.

Father gave us love and good guidance throughout his life with us. He and I had deferent perception about western Education and culture but we reconciled after my completing primary school at Kinte Kunda.

My father's experience from the hands of colonials made him never to entertain idea of his progeny deviating from the farmers' mould. Nor would he allow me pursue Western Education and ideology, which at the time was alien to my father and his peers.

He once told me: Son, my wish for you is to be a hard working good farmer and not indulge in the quagmire and sleaze world of spin-doctors. I do not want you tinkering with ideology that would infuse into you wrong philosophies about life and God. My father came from a different generation with totally different perceptions about invaders ruling them. Let us for a moment step into their shoes to find out why the resistance for their progeny to attend school. In my father's days men believed in God, the sanctity of life and peaceful coexistence of the communities they lived.

About the invading longhaired men he calls devils, father said: "Son the way these men, meaning the colonialist, took over our countries can only be the work of the devil. They came from the blue sea and seized our land and minerals, and remaining on the best parts while leaving us the worst places to farm and for our animals to grace. To pour oil on fire they requested that we change our religions and ways to their dark and indiscipline life styles.

To top up, our people were forced to live under laws promulgated by the invaders on top of which we must pay to learn their languages while they make systemic concerted efforts to distorted and destroy everything that was dear to us. They massacred, disgraced, and dethroned all our kings and chiefs.

These shameful acts were reinforced with policies of divide and rule by pitting tribe against tribe and even bribing those bad elements willing to do their dirty work. Wages paid to workers were not worth the coin they were minted on.

They made certain no organization, political or professional civil service existed in our countries". He said, "They filled the jails with those of us who refused to be indoctrinated or accept the supremacy of the foreign invaders.

So Son, because of kind-heartedness and gentled nature of the African our ways are undermined and thrown out by invaders who replaced it with greed, unkindness, spin-doctoring, and lack of respect for man and nature. He concluded by saying, these are just a few reasons why I would not let my blood attend school".

The above is a pinhole view of father's radicalism and patriotic views. He did recap late later in his old age and finally gave full blessings to my efforts and future goals. He passed away peacefully to his maker in 1991 while I was a trainee doctor doing my clinical clerkship rotation at Colchester General Hospital in Colchester, Essex County, England.

Notices no matter how simple were just bundles of scribbles on worthless paper to the farmer. The illiterates who cannot decipher the prints are cheated of their rights and land.

I was not going to be among those who cannot decipher the print and hence found my way to Kinte Kunda Primary School where I met with the head Master, Mr. Louis Albert Bouvier, who hails from Banjul, our capital city.

This benevolent teacher was my first real contact with Western Education and we gelled instantly and became inseparable. He allowed me to stay at his home and treated me as his own son. He was kind and firm and wasted no time teaching me about life and on how to compete without strangulating the competitor.

Dr. Alhasan S. Ceesay holding Africa

He told me repeatedly that competition was a healthy fund and stressed that one must be honest and have integrity and tolerance in life. He counselled hard work at everything one did. Above all, it was incumbent on me to have faith and to serve God daily, if not more but never less. Also he allowed me all the freedom a growing child needed without pampering me.

He did lay certain straightforward and simple rules for me. I was to study at a designated time, return home in time whenever I went into town, unless given an extension by him, and to be in bed by 10:00 pm, with lights off whether sleepy or not. He insisted that I perform my five daily prayers as expected of my religion even though he was devoured Catholic.

Mr. Bouvier would only help with my homework when he felt that I have done my best at it and that I was not trying to have him do the work. Otherwise, he would let me go and make a fool of myself before the class before I deserve his coveted help.

Hash you think but this strict beginning or treatment, as you would call it, made me do well at school and do things with confidence independently at very tender age.

Dr. Alhasan Sisawo Ceesay, MD

I remain profoundly grateful to Mr. Louis Albert Bouvier for being educational springboard, for being a sincere and true friend and mentor. Something said by Francis Farmer summed up the relationship between L. A. Bouvier and me.

She said, "To have a good friend is the purest of all God' gifts, for it is a love that has no exchange of payments. It is not inherited, as with family. It is not compelling, as with a child. And it has no means of physical pleasures, as with a mate. It is, therefore, an indescribable bond that brings with it a far deeper devotion than others".

Mr. L. A Bouvier continued to help and mold my academic life until when I started Armitage School in 1957. Leaving a friend like Mr. Bouvier was difficult and emotional for both of us. We have become one and are now to say farewell and perhaps separate forever.

He prepared me well but like any parent or true friend he worried about the difficulties that lay ahead. I just wished they had transferred him with me to Armitage. On the day I boarded the land rover to Armitage tears rundown Mr. Bouvier's cheeks and mother turned her head away to hide her own.

Son of the Savannah

L. A. Bouvier was my best friend, after the loss of my twin brother, fate had it that I was now about to be far away from all I knew and loved. Mr. L. A. Bouvier kept cautioning me to, "keep your head up and do your school works. You have never been a failure, and even if such a sad experience occurs, keep trying over and over to overcome it.

We send you to Armitage with prayers, pride and above all with our deepest love. May God keep you in good health. Goodbye, Mr. Ceesay." It was very moving for this was the first time he addressed me as Mr. Ceesay. We boarded the Land Rover and as it started to move Bouvier followed for some distance exhorting me not to fear to ask for help when need arose. He kept saying he would gladly help or would ask my parents to pitch in whenever possible.

Mr. L. A. Bouvier and I kept in touch despite the distance poor mail service of those days. The link continued while I was in the USA. I lost my friend in a motorcar accident, six year before returning from America in 1974. His vehicle is said to have ran off the road went over a hill. Another part of me went with him. The evil that men do lives after them and the good is interred with their bodies.

Dr. Alhasan Sisawo Ceesay, MD

Well rest assured that L. A. Bouvier's good deeds did remain alive and intact on earth. At Armitage it was a newly qualified teaches from Kaur, Mr. Keko B. A. Manneh, who then doubled as our class' English and Mathematic teacher that filled in gap left by my leaving L. A. Bouvier at Kinte Kunda.

He was soft-spoken Chaucerian, a nickname we gave him because he crammed the entire work of Chaucer. He too loved me and was a good guide at Arbitrage. I am grateful for encouragement and help he gave and for really being there when I needed an honest person to open up to about difficulty or academic aspiration. I left for New York on the 24 August 1967 and arrived at Alpena Michigan 1:30 Am on the 25 August 1967.

Mr. Henry V. Vali, a counselor and foreign student advisor at Alpena Community College, was at the bus station to pick me. After the formality of welcoming to Alpena he drove me to 251 Washington Avenue the home of Mr. Howard Riggs where it had been agreed I stay until start of the semester in September before moving to Russell Wilson Hall at the Alpena Community College campus. Not surprising Mr. Vali and I became friends and remained so ever since.

Son of the Savannah

Mr. Howard Riggs and family welcomed me home as late as it was on that glorious day when I set foot in Michigan. They were all delighted to have me in their lovely home and they gave me princely meal to nourish my body and milk to quench my thirst.

Howard owned Ice-Cream Pallor down Town. He was very modest, delightful man and above all a very generous person. Soon Mr. and Mrs. Riggs became mom and dad throughout my American stay for their overwhelmingly kind people deserving such salutation from a poor villager.

Howard's warmth and generosity to other made his family unique company to foreign students coming to Alpena. The Riggs were the ideal Americans to me. They were average working family who readily shared the little bit God gave them with others less fortunate. I remained grateful to these kind-hearted friends.

Mr. Valli and Mr. Thomas Ritter, Director of Foreign students at Alpena Community College, and I met several time to discuss my financial nightmare. Mr. Ritter was too concerned that the college might face INS censor if he allowed my staying without a sponsor or means to pay fees and cater for myself.

Dr. Alhasan Sisawo Ceesay, MD

He was adamant and made it very clear to me that failure to get help for the first semester will leave him with no other option but to advise the immigration to consider deporting proceedings against me.

He gave a week ultimatum for me to sort things out before our next meeting 18 September 1967. Copies of letters from my future sponsor, Mr. Isidor Gold, never move or evoke sympathy from him as he epidermises a true inelastic bureaucrat.

Mr. Henry V. Valli convinced Mr. Thomas Ritter to hold on while get in touch with some residents about my case. He was on the telephone to different would be possible sympathizers to my cause.

Most of who agreed to contribute toward the cost of my first semester at Alpena Community College. Mr. Valli also spoke to the president of the college in my behalf to prevent Mr. Ritter from hastily and unilaterally contacting the INS for frivolous fears in his head. My plight soon became a house whole affair and many residents pitched in to help resolve the case.

Son of the savannah

The appeal by Mr. Henry Valli and Mrs. Viola Glennie snowballed letting me start my first semester at Alpena Community College, Alpena, Michigan. Fr. John miller at St. Bernard Rectory in Alpena not only lent me $250 but evangelized my state in every sermon for three weeks netting me much needed financial help. God bless his heart. He left Alpena before my transfer to Olivet College in Olivet Michigan in 1979.

Judge Philip Glennie was head of the 26th circuit Court of Michigan at the time. His wife, Mrs. Viola Gennie, was professor of foreign language at Alpena Community College. Both not only contributed substantial amounts towards my tuition but also became my adopted parents in Alpena. They continued to link with me like wise support my goal until their return to heaven in the late nineties.

I remember these friends with joy mingled with sadness that they are not here to share reward they showed but also I remember them with intense gratitude for role and kindness shown me while a student at Alpena Community College, Alpena, Michigan, USA.

Dr. Alhasan Sisawo Ceesay, MD

In another vein Alpena Community College gave me part time job at the Library and a summer job at the Salmon Experimental Fish hatchery. Thanks to grand efforts of Mr. Henry V. Valli and residents of Alpena I was able to overcome the financial crisis of my first semester at the college.

I met Mr. Cloyd Ramsey while seeking a summer job at the Medical Arts Clinic in Alpena. He was then manager of the unit at the time. Upon hearing my plight he promised to see what he could do even though the clinic itself had no jobs openings for that summer. I left him impressed and very moved by what he heard.

He too became an integral part of my time and sojourner in America than any through contributions and loans he took from the Alpena bank in my behalf to support my studies throughout my stay in the USA and short stay in Liberia, West Africa.

It was through kindness of Mr. Ramsey and his sponsorship that enabled Michigan Technological University at Houghton to accept me do a Masters program in Biological Sciences from 1971 to 1973.

L – R: Dr. Alhasan Ceesay, Prof. Sulayman Nyang, Mr. Clloyd Ramsey and Prof. Francis Conti

Dr. Alhasan Sisawo Ceesay, MD

It was Mr. Cloyd Ramsey who came to my rescuer when things went very bad and unbearable and practically unsafe for me after the military coup d'etat against William Tolbert' administration of Liberia in 1981. He provided a round trip Air ticket to the USA and supporting it with invitation for me as their guest at Sandusky, Michigan December 1981.

The invitation secured me a B-2 Visa to Detroit, Michigan. I arrived in New York 1:15 pm 20 December 1981. I prayed on disembarking and I was grateful and thankful to God and Cloyd Ramsey having set foot once more on US soil. I thank Cloyd ceaselessly in my heart for having helped me escape to America despite the ignominy of being in exile and to seek asylum soon.

I caught my flight to Detroit, Michigan around 3:45 pm same day. The Ramseys were at the Detroit Metropolitan International arrivals terminal waiting to receive me. They must have noted the fatigue in my face, if not the sorrow of leaving my beloved Gambia and people behind for an indefinite time. They welcomed me graciously and we headed for Sandusky, a small village in Michigan. I therein and then became part of the Ramsey family.

Son of the savannah

Life has it that when some of us were created the mould broke. Most give their time and money to their own families or to work that brings them some happiness and some money. Cloyd Ramsey is among a few who give themselves wholly and unselfishly to others.

I can never be able to repay or tell how devoted Ramsey is in sharing life with the needy unless you meet him. In brief, Mr. Ramsey and wife Narrate fed and sheltered me when I needed food and place to stay until I get my feet back on earth.

He was my salvation voice in the wilderness of life's rugged road. I stayed as their guest in Sandusky until it was time to seek asylum at the Immigration and Nationality Service (INS) in Detroit. There was no other situation less tense and so empty of hope than this next phase in my life.

Life became an abyss of despair which only God and good friends, like the Ramseys, pulled me out from underneath. Shakespeare said, "Between the acting of a dreadful thing and the first motion; All the interim is like a phantasm, or a hideous dream. The genius and mortals instruments like to a little kingdom, suffers then the nature of an insurrection."

Dr. Alhasan Sisawo Ceesay, MD

Indeed an insurrection has been going on in my head during those horrible days of the coup d'etat of April 15th 1980 I became aware of the need to muster courage, strength and endurance to prepare myself for the coming exile days and form it may take.

Again, Mr. Ramsey contacted the Gambia several time to no avail to verify and correct a possible misunderstanding that may have occurred. Several friends and legislators Ramsey contacted advised that I seek asylum from the INS. Senator Carl Levin sent us a package of three copies of Form 1-589 for my use on 6th January 1982.

We took the bull by the horns, completed the forms and Ramsey and I proceeded to INS office at Mount Elliot Street, Detroit, Michigan on the 22nd February 1982, were I was subsequently interviewed separately and told action will be rendered in four months earliest.

If wishes were horses beggars would gallop to heaven for it took well more than eight months before any reply came and only after numerous INS court hearings did we get some semblance of partial positive direction. The final act was left with the State Department and vice president's office.

Son of the Savannah

Things were so delayed and difficult that I asked Ramsey to take me to the Catholic Mission for me to seek Sanctuary or more public help and support. We landed at St. Paul's' Cathedral, Diocese of Michigan, where Hugh Davis led me to the refugee office of the Diocese.

On hearing my story the refugee co-coordinator, Mrs. Patricia Koblinsky called rev. Hugh C. White, advisor to the reigning Bishop of the Diocese, Bishop Coleman Mcgehee Jr. The Diocese received and let me stay at 44 Ledyard Street in Detroit. In the mean time Ramsey sent the following appeal to the INS office at Mount Elliot in Detroit, Michigan:

TO WHOM IT MAY CONCERN

This letter is to acknowledge my association with Alhasan Ceesay, over a period of fifteen years. During that time I have found him to be a young man of very high ideals. His only interest in life has been to obtain an education and return to serve his home country and help his people.

I have personally invested thousands of dollars in Alhasan Ceesay because it seemed to me to be a very efficient way to help the impoverished people from his country that has had a great deal less than I have.

Dr. Alhasan Sisawo Ceesay, MD

If anyone were to follow the course of his life, he would see that his motives most certainly were not to simply escape the futility of his home country and live that, good life here. There is no doubt in my mind that the dangers that he describes do exist for him.

Even if these were less than perfect proof, would you like to take the chance of being wrong and find out that he had been imprison or worse killed for no reason at all?

Please save this man. If you cannot do it for his sake, then consider the investment made by concerned individuals, other organizations and myself. Thank you for your serious considerations of this matter. Signed: Cloyd Ramsey, Sandusky, Michigan, USA

My next Alpena Samaritan and brother in Chris as well as profession was Dr. Charles T. Egli, who I met almost about the same time I did with Ramsey. He was a Surgeon working for the Medical Arts Clinic at the time of our meeting. He came into the radar after a speech I gave to the Alpena Medical Association.

He too has contributed prominently and was instrumental in having the medical Association comes to my aid with a donation of $400 towards my second semester fees at Alpena Community College.

Son of the savannah

By this miracle I was able to complete payment for the second semester at college. Charles, as he prefers being called, is a surgeon and devoted Christian who also became very close friend and had done a lot to encourage my efforts.

His rallying for assistance continued throughout his days at the Medical Arts Clinic. For you to note Dr. Egli's closeness here is a letter he sent in my behalf during my petitioning for asylum in the USA. It read:

Medical Arts Clinic

Alpena, Michigan

November 14, 1986

RE: Deportation Notice on Alhasan Ceesay

Dear Senator Levin,

Alhasan Ceeesay was a college student in Alpena many years ago when I first met him and was very much impressed by his sincerity and enthusiasm. He went onto graduate school at Michigan Technological University in Houghton, Michigan, in hopes of getting into medical school.

Dr. Alhasan Sisawo Ceesay, MD

He tried very hard to get into medical school in Africa. He was receiving no support from his own country because it considered him a political agitator and tribalist. Alhasan Ceesay on his own initiative was able to get into medical school in Monrovia Liberia and succeeded in taking two years medical education before he fled for safety to the USA. He later sought political asylum in the USA for fear of persecution due to the aftermath of an attempted coup in July 181.

It has always been his desire to complete his medical training and return to the Gambia when the climate warrants. For almost five years now, Alhasan has been trying to receive asylum, during which time his chances at medical school are affected. Most recently he received a letter from INS judge ordering his deportation. The deportation of Alhasan Ceesay back to the Gambia would result in his certain death or imprisonment and would constitute another tragedy in the way our government handles people like Alhasan. In a country where there are so many illegal aliens it seems that there must be some place for one more refugee. I beg you to personally consider Alhasan Ceesay's case.

Sincerely

Dr. Charles T. Egli, MD

Son of the savannah

Mr. Homer Sheppard, resident of Flint Michigan, was also very kind to me while at Flint. He offered to lodge me during the summer of 1969 on securing a full time job at the St. Joseph Hospital on Flint, Michigan as nurse assistant.

Homer and wife offered to help defray rent expenses, which were taking a quarter of my earnings. With this help I was able to return to Alpena Community College at the end of the summer and pay my dorm and food bills and still had some pocket money to buy pens and other sundries during the semester.

God blesses his heart. We lost contact since my return to Africa. All letters to his address were redirected, as addressee no longer leaves here. Bishop Coleman McGehee had already blessed efforts of the hastily formed CEESAY COMMITTEE.

It became the Adhoc committee and my Pegasus wing. Like any normal human gatherings we had our different ideas as to how to approach the asylum problem but all of it steered towards or sought better ways to meet the challenges and enigma about to end all that I stood for and worked hard for in life. The brain storming sessions were very pragmatic if not practical and well-intended discussions.

Dr. Alhasan Sisawo Ceesay, MD

One of the exploratory searches for solutions led us to Mayor Harvey Sloan of Louisville, Kentucky. I met Mayor Sloan in 1976 when I was trying to get into medical school at the University of Louisville. Also we used to write each other while I was in Monrovia, Liberia, West Africa. I was invited to his office early February 1983, and was given opportunity to talk with key aids at the Louisville City Hall while he attended other state affairs.

His executive aids, Sharon Wilbert and Mrs. Blanche reviewed my case along with information already in my file open in my name. They concluded that I did deserve help and I was asked to speak to Mrs. Joyce J. Rayzer, Director, and Health Affairs for the Mayor. Joyce contacted the Dean of the Medical School and gave him an in-depth briefing of my background and precarious situation I was faced with. Two weeks later on February 28th 1983, I received the following letter from Joyce in behalf of Mayor Harvey Sloan. It read thus:

Office of the Director of Safety

City Hall

Louisville, Kentucky 40202

28 February 1983

Son of the Savannah

Dear Mr. Ceesay,

It appears, as the old saying goes, that I have good news and bad news. I have been in contact with the University Of Louisville School Of Medicine with regards to your admission at the fall term. I have spoken to Dr. Donald Kemetz, Dean of the Medical School, and Mr. Harold Adams, Special Assistance to the president of the University of Louisville.

Both of these administrators upon reviewing the information you sent me feel that you are a very good candidate for the minority admission program. There is however, one issue, which must be resolved favourably before your admission to medical school, or the financing and packaging necessary to begging this endeavour can be given serious considerations.

The issue, which must be resolved, is the financial determination base on whether you would be granted asylum in the country. Without the asylum being granted and hence financial aid the university cannot proceed with your request for admission this fall because your legal status would be too tenuous for them to invest hard cash in your future medical development under such nebulous state.

Dr. Alhasan Sisawo Ceesay, MD

It appears that you must begin medical school anew. The two years completed at Liberia, cannot be accepted for transfer. You will start as freshman upon being granted asylum in USA. Again, try and find resolution to granting you asylum.

I have been assured that everything that can be done for you will be done immediately upon a favourable notice of your asylum. Everybody in the Mayor's office says hello, and we are sending you our prayers.

Sincerely

Joyce J. Rayzer

Director, Health Affairs

This was the impact Mayor Harvey Sloan had. In addition Mayor Harvey Sloan sent the following directly from his desk to the INS pleasing for them to grant me asylum.

City Hall

Office of the Mayor

Louisville, KY 40202

November 7, 1983

Son of the Savannah

Alhasan S. Ceesay of the Gambia has contacted this office in an effort to gain political asylum in other to complete his medical education at the University of Louisville. I know that he is dedicated individual and is more desirous of providing needed medical aid to his fellow man. Mr. Ceesay petitioned for political asylum in February 22, 1982 due to a purge, which followed a failed coup in the Gambia.

The Medical school at the university of Louisville is currently processing his application for the 1984/85 academic years. It would be most helpful if you could assist him in expediting his papers. He will not be admitted unless a written statement confirming his residency status is available.

Since he has already lost two years awaiting residency confirmation, it would be deeply appreciated if you could assist this young man in any way possible. If my staff or I can be any further assistance in the matter, please do not hesitate to contact this office.

Sincerely

Harvey L Sloan

Mayor Louisville

Dr. Alhasan Sisawo Ceesay, MD

Let us for a moment revert to Bishop Coleman McGehee at the Episcopal Diocese of Michigan in Detroit Michigan. Below is letter sent to the INS director, Edwin Chauvin at Mount Elliot in Detroit, Michigan.

Office of the Bishop

4800 Woodward Avenue

Detroit, Michigan 48201

24 October 1983

Dear Mr. Chauvin,

As Bishop for the Episcopal diocese of Michigan, located in Detroit, Michigan, I write you this letter on behalf of Alhasan S. Ceesay, a petitioner for political asylum in the United States.

As you may note from the file Mr. Ceesay seeks political asylum base on his fear of political persecution and danger to his physical safety and well being by the government, were he to be returned by the INS to his country the Gambia.

Mr. Ceesay's life will disclose to you, he was active opponent of the political regime in the Gambia.

Son of the savannah

After protesting incarceration of his friends, Mr. Ceesay was placed on a list of individuals who were allegedly involved in criminal activity and who were involved with the Movement for Justice in Africa (MOJA) and were sought for interrogation by the Gambia government.

The Gambia government has singled our Mr. Ceesay because of his political opposition and has prevented him from continuing his medical education in Liberia by cutting off his financial assistance and by asking the Liberian government to return Mr. Ceesay to the Gambia.

I am personally acquainted with Mr. Ceesay, and believe him to be an individual who is worthy of support of the Episcopal Dioceses of Michigan. I feel that it took great courage for Mr. Ceesay to stand up for human rights and to publicly oppose the political regime in the Gambia.

I am convinced that Mr. Ceesay is an altruistic individual who deserves to pursue his medical training to benefit, both in the United States and perhaps elsewhere, those individuals who might be helped by his medical ability.

Dr. Alhasan Sisawo Ceesay, MD

Mr. Ceesay has already establish his medical science aptitude in his studies at Medical School in Liberia, and he has applied to and been accepted by the School of Medicine at the University of Louisville, Kentucky, with tuition to be paid by that institution, upon his authorization to remain in the United States.

Mr. Ceesay has also sought authorization to engage in employment pending the outcome of his asylum request, he proposes to assist in medical research at the university should his employment authorization be granted by your office.

Therefore, on behalf of Mr. Ceesay as well as the members of my Diocese, I would urge you to give favorable consideration to Mr. Ceesay's petition and expedite his request for employment and his political asylum petition in every possible way so that his efforts to enter the University of Louisville School of Medicine may not be delayed any longer than may be necessary by legal and administrative procedures which you office follows.

 Please feel free to contact me if I can be of any assistance in helping you to reach your determination on this matter.

I fervently believed that, upon your investigation of Mr. Ceesay's case, you would reach the conclusions that he would be an asset to the United States, and that his fears as to his persecution and personal safety should he return to the Gambia, have firm foundation in fact.

Very truly yours

(The Rt. Rev.) H. Coleman McGehee, Jr.

Bishop of Michigan

The Bishop of Michigan, H. Coleman McGehee followed the above with a letter to then vice president George Bush Sr. Who sent the following tars reply.

The Vice President

Washington, D. C

April 25, 1984

Dear Rev. McGehee,

Thank you for your recent letter concerning Alhasan S. Ceesay. It was thoughtful of you to write and I appreciate your having taken the time to bring Mr. Ceesay's case to my attention. I have asked the State Department to review all asylum cases and human rights violations, which are brought to my attention.

I have, therefore shared your letter and the enclosures with officials at the Department of State and asked that they review Mr. Ceesay's request and write to you directly. I have also asked that a copy of their response be forwarded to my office. With best wishes.

Sincerely

George Bush

Bishop McGehhee, Bishop Mason, Rev. Hugh C. white, Rev. David Brower, Rev. Bill Woods, Rev. Virgil Jones, and Rev. Mark D. Meyer all touched my heart in similar fashions Hence here is my collective feeling and experience in a nut shell about these devoted men of Christ.

All of the priests lived in Detroit, Michigan except Rev. Mark D. Meyer, who lived in Planes view, Texas, USA. I lived with Rev. Mark Meyer in 1989 after hurricane Hugo devastated our campus at Montserrat, West Indies. The rest of the above I met while trying to defray deportation notice from the INS. Those were challenging and nerving political moments for m family and I.

Son of the Savannah

These men of God never docked when told about my nightmare. These true believers became unique brothers I would like to share few outstanding things they did in style engraved in simple devotion to Christ's dictum.

I write because these men impressed me in their interpretations and devotion to the Gospel of Christ. Hence forgive me if I became a bit sentimental in relaying help they gave to me at various challenging times of my life.

They were personal pastors for me. These were the beacon of hope and faith that stood by me when it was all doom and gloomy for me. They were simple people, humble ones at that, I can confide with, debate with, and had shoulders on which to cry my heart out without being embarrassed and above all expect a little prayer at the end of it.

Then guess what? We would be on tract trying to get hold of friends of theirs and people that might lighten my burden. Their devotion to justice and fairness was magnanimous and are my brothers in Christ. Rev. Mark Meyer, on being told the hardship I endured in Montserrat from hurricane Hugo gave me a room and gifts more than ten thousand u.s. dollars to help me complete my pre-clinics at the American University School of Medicine.

Dr. Alhasan Sisawo Ceesay, MD

I learnt from these men of God that there is a special strength that can sustain us through almost any difficulty. That strength comes from God and from kind hearts like these Samaritans of good will. The strength comes from partly within but even more, it comes from faith and love of those close to us.

These men gave themselves wholly and as unselfishly to others in need when I met them at the Episcopalian diocese of Michigan. They devoted time to my cause and dropped selfish interests aside to help me fight my case against the INS while I was up to my neck in legal and political mud.

I found nothing in these men but admirable integrity, honesty and unswerving commitment to leading life devoted to God, the Bible and in helping the downtrodden. I always feel elated whenever I get chance to speak to these kind hearts from afar.

Meeting them makes me feel reunited with my best friends. I rather have a million more like then than multi millionaires that do not care about the plight of the common man. Again, I applaud contribution and friendship these men touched my heart and life with. God blesses them.

My family, villagers and I are extremely indebted to them. These men translated their concerns, and love of humanity and continued to be my good Samaritans and a bridge over trouble waters. These believe in the worthiness and sanctity of life.

And above all they ascribe to the power of knowledge and justice over ignorance. We look forward to the day we can serenade them amongst us in the smiling coast of the Gambia. We pray they keep fit to be able to join us in the opening ceremony of the Manding Medical Centre at Njawara village, the Gambia, West Africa.

These men translated their deep faith, concerns, and love of humanity. I opted to do my clinical rotations in Colchester, Essex, UK in 1990 and chanced to meet the Robinson's. Keith Robinson vested my newly born baby girl, Famatanding Ceesay, at the Colchester County Hospital, which marked our first meeting.

This slightly shy bloke impressed me a lot. He was all smiles and fund. He titled the little ears of my daughter and told her not to be as bad as her daddy. We all laughed over it. We from that moment liked each other and he became one of my inseparable unique Brits.

Keith and wife would visit the Gambia and my girls loved them to bits. Not for the presents he takes to them each time but because of his amiable personality, altruistic, very caring human he is. He had spent boxes of monetary aid towards my NGO, Manding Medical Centre at Njawara village, and the Gambia.

On the forming of the Friends Manding Charitable Trust, he was unanimously voted chairman of the charity by the members. He had since inspiration of the Friends of Manding Charitable Trust worn the cap admirably and did a job well done for the charity.

Also he had been instrumental in the Gambibazaar held every fortnight in Colchester to help raise funds for Manding Medical Centre's goals back in the Gambia. He is committed to seeing the centre come to fruition for the villagers of the Gambia and any that would need its service.

Personally, he and his wife had been my lifeline and support. They have always come to my aid the call of expectation and I remain profoundly grateful to him and his wife Lorna V. Robinson. Ten years ago I was on the verge of preparing becoming a consultant and return to serve the Gambia.

Son of the Savannah

Today an untold anguish my life went through in these years was dampened by kindness of Lorna and Keith Robinson and many other kind and generous Brits. They are my Colchester Samaritans and Njawara villager's angels with golden hearts.

We are working hard to seeing that Manding Medical center transcends the dream it was to reality for the Lower Badibou region. Its service is much needed by the villagers. God blesses their hearts.

In Manchester many helped but few match Elhaj Asfaque Ahammed, Neville Brown, Kofi Awudo and Ahmed Nizami. Elh. Asfaque Ahammed is proprietor of Punjab Collection located at Wilmslow Road in Manchester. A lot has already been revealed about the kindness and generosity of this gentile heart and family in my first book, "The legend again all odds."

Ishfaque Ahammed has since my early days in Manchester to today been benevolent towards me. He gives me food and money any time he thinks or feels that I am on the brink of collapsing because of joblessness, hunger, and worries about the state of my equally beleaguered family back home. Only God can reward such humble good people.

Dr. Alhasan Sisawo Ceesay, MD

I first met Neville in Montserrat, West Indies, while I was a medical student at the American University of the Caribbean. We have ever since been cordial and upon finding me out in Manchester he had steadfastly kept that friendship ablaze.

He in various ways would come to my aid with small but significant donations at the time. He even helped in securing a job at Belfry House Hotel at Hands Forth in 2006. He is kind-hearted fellow and my Montserrat. Kofi Awudo is Toggles gentleman I also met through his link with Neville Brown.

He turned to be very kind and generous to me. He bought me shoes and shirts to allow me start work at the above hotel. Years later on my return from Glasgow, Scotland he was the one that lodged me free of charge for three winter months. He is of exceptional quality and humane person. I remain grateful both fellows.

I met Mr. Ahamed Nizami in 2008, an angel in human flesh, at Waseem's work place in Manchester. This lawyer turned Editor and I gelled from that hour to today. He is currently the Chief Editor of the Khalish Magazine, an Urdu language magazine in UK and worldwide. He also doubles as one of the Pakistani group leader in Manchester. On knowing my predicaments his benevolence surfaced.

There nod then he promised to help me with some the problems pulling me down and also indicated interest in helping my NGO Manding Medical Centre get financial aid to get a head start on the provision of its goals for the villagers.

In addition he proposed a fun raising idea using his medium and other avenues that may come to light. We tentatively initiated, depending on approval and provisos set by Keith Robinson, Chairman of Friends of Manding Charitable Trust in Colchester been met, formation of the Manchester Manding Medical Center Annex to be office at 9 knowley Street in Manchester.

To further demonstrate his kindness and interest in my goal Ahmed Nizami donated fees for all three PLAB exams I took in 2009. Gentle hearts like Ganem Hadied and others felt sorry that my life became an unkind and rough ride for me. He said, "Ceesay, I wish I can help more to get you out of the limbo you found yourself. Just believe in God and this pain will one day pass like history."

Mahmud Adam also marched Ganem's effort by collecting money from the Liverpool mosque. Both monies were used for my exam fees and for which kindness I remain eternally grateful to all donors.

Mohamed Salam of Greenhey business in Manchester was another Good Samaritan that came to my aid when I was left to sleep in cold weather at Alexandra Park. Upon contacting him he kindly offered me room in one of his flats in Manchester.

 He was very kind and generous towards me. We have many times prayed together for my eventual breaking out of nightmarish bad luck life had been to me in recent times. Last but not the least is Sami Bati from Algeria who I stayed with at 245 Great Western Street and who relentlessly called and ask people and friends to come to aid.

He raised a bundle to help me pay school fees for my daughters in the Gambia and feed my bones. My brother Abdullah Hashim and wife Asiya Qadri were very kind Bangladesh cum Pakistani couple I met during the most challenging times of my life.

Their kindness is yet to be matched by their peers. I met the couple while sleeping rough in the street of Manchester as Mohamed Salam' offer of a place came to an abrupt end.

Son of the Savannah

The place was rented to a family leaving me homeless with no place to go except spend the nights at cold and treacherous Alexandra Park. It was very risky but being jobless it was the only option left to me. Hence, it was a miracle when this God fearing Good Samaritan couple came to my rescue.

They not only lodged me temporally at their other flat at 2 Sway field in Manchester but also continued to shower me with gifts and food. I certainly look forward to hosting and having my villagers and family serenade this unusually kind and generous couple from Bangladesh.

Yankuba Samateh and dear friend Abdinisir Hassan deserve a mention with gratitude and thanks for kindness and generosity they showered me with during these dark days and for constantly reminding me that I am more than capable of bringing my dream to fruition for the villagers.

Mrs. Roheyata Corr-Sey, a cousin, remained the most supportive and one that kept encouraging me more than any family member had done during this sojourn of mine. God blesses her and her family. I look forward to being able to thank her in person for insisting that blood is thicker than water and for being with me in thick and thin of this murderous trail.

Dr. Alhasan Sisawo Ceesay, MD

I just have to have continued faith; confidence to do it and the universe will cooperate to justify these days difficulty. My life being as mythical as Pelebstine fever, it was full of ups and downs and again it was Ahamed Nizami who offered to lodge me when I was asked to leave my previous address where I was renting. His kindness is phenomenal and transience's mortals.

I look forward to him being my guest in the Gambia. Worth mentioning is Abdullah Shahim, a young Bangladeshi fellow who practiced his believe that we are all God's children and do need to help the miskin whenever we can.

He has graced my life with kindness and brotherhood that any human being yearns to get. He and his wife Asiya Padri have been one of the bright experiences of my UK sojourn. God bless their hearts. Asiya is a shining beauty and sunshine of Abdullah Shahim.

Each day became a specific thrill that lead to that exhilarating moment of victory for mankind. It was a hard challenge and a march placed before me. It is a march I will pursue towards the day I would once again be able to serve the Gambia as a physician.

Son of the savannah

Friends such as Lorna Robinson, Eliza Jones, Mahmud Adam, Ganem Hadied, Abdinnisir, Faisal, Yusuf Ali, Ishfaque Ahmed, Ahmed Nizami, Abdullah Shahim, and countless angels all suffered my pain and felt way into my heart through compassion as I plied through financial inadequacies.

Angels like Faisal, Abdul Rhaseed, Abdinnisir, Yusuf Ali, and Mahmud Adam deserved to be classed as paragons of kindness. These Somalis are among many who refused to let me bit the dust because of foot dragging visa problem. They encouraged by sharing food and they had with me and made certain that I persevere for a bright day for family and country.

These are people who help lift my feet when my wings could not remember how to fly away from hardship. Faisal would on weekends prepare hot and well spiced Spaghetti and meat, or buy food for me from the next door restraint. Abdinnisir Hassan in almost tearful manner would push me into going to get food.

On top of this generosity these folks let me stay in their flat at 284 Great Western Street, Manchester while my lawyer fight not only to untangle but to get the Home office act on change of status request I made to that office back in 2004.

Dr. Alhasan Sisawo Ceesay, MD

I feel favoured, if not blessed having to face these inhuman challenges without losing my sanity. Being in the belly of a ferocious beast is more comfortable than life I am currently saddled. I feel like being at the interface between Purgatory and hell on earth.

Simply put, my experience was no domain for the weak. The dilemma in this life remains ceaselessly changing. These few, this band of altruistic brothers kept me going through many a dark hour of my life in America and Great Britain.

They stood tall for me among many in caring for the plight of those who they never met in poverty stricken parts of the world. Friends like these are angels who lift us to our feet when our wings have trouble remembering how to fly.

In this almost inhospitable life friends like these are a great gift indeed. Tinged with trepidations for what the future can sing I picked up courage and inspiration knowing that good comes out of fighting for what one believes in.

Life has taught me how to look after myself and that things do not just happen, people make it happen. And so the villagers and I appeal for your help and participation with Manding Medical Centre.

Son of the savannah

Together we can walk on water and make this dream of providing medical aid to villages become worthy cause for generations. I have learnt not to rest on my oars else I fall into a deep and turbulent sea of troubles.

I have to keep running in order to be with the best or where I am. I will continue to not only learn to improve my performance but to work hard to see that this dream of providing a much needed medical aid to villagers is brought to fruition.

Dalliance said, "Say of me what you will and the morrow will judge you, and your words shall be a witness before its judgment and a testimony before its justice. I came to say a word and I shall utter it.

Should death take me ere I give voice the morrow shall utter it. That which alone I do today shall be proclaimed before the people in the days to come."

Chapter 17

I REST MY CASE

Paul in a letter to Timothy 2 said, "I have fought a good fight, I have finished my course, and I have kept the faith." I hand this work for publication for you to be judge of the ravages of the years and how my life was that of extreme ups and downs.

In reality, I am very grateful to God even though my life met with various misfortunes, the most unbearable being the delay in my becoming a physician.

My life as witnessed in these pages was an assembly of trials and tribulation emanating from roadblocks placed on my path by inhuman laws and unfortunate dark circumstances.

Life has taught me to submit to divine decrees, whatever they may be from God. I feel on the whole overly rewarded and delivered even though I had no family here in England nor was I as lucky as others who can feel and experience the warmth of their wives and children on daily basis.

I succumbed to it as the way things were going to be for me and lived with this state of affairs while in Manchester, England. I experienced various turns of fate, enough for ten elephant loads, while on the little moat of the silver sea called England.

Son of the Savannah

With my travels I was able to see Europe, the Americas and have learnt a great deal from it as well as experienced numerous unforeseen adventures thrown on my path. My life in England was pain; fear of deportation, hunger, extreme poverty due to joblessness, solitude and missing my wife and children I loved dearly.

I had a huge sense of duty in relation to the villagers and was not ready to fail them because of personal comfort or pleasures. Consequently Manding Medical Centre and benefits to be accrued from it became my most if not the only occupation and direction in life.

Here is Manding Medical Centre if managed well it will do justice to rural health service for the next generation of Gambians to build upon. The medical centre is now a recognized charity in both the United Kingdom and America. I am committed to serve the villagers so that life of the children and young people would be better than mine when I was young.

I hope Manding Medical Centre becomes a model testimony of the boy from Njawara village who doggedly struggled to become a doctor and despite various twists of life is able to provide medical aid and service to villagers in rural Gambia.

May be this will strengthen some other fellow to strive to do better than I did to bring health and happiness to the region. I hope my adventure persuades youngsters that man is capable of a lot more than he thinks he is capable of.

Dr. Alhasan Sisawo Ceesay, MD

Our footprints must be inspirational to give heart to new coming Gambian generations. Twenty years ago none would dream of thinking me becoming an author or to challenge powers as I did in this little frame and life of mine. I met a beautiful Maraka girl while I was in Monrovia, Liberia, West Africa.

Fatou Koma is daughter of Elhaj Ansuman Koma and Jalian Ture of Kindia from Guinea Conakry. Her positive attitudes towards me lead our meeting on weekends at Cousin Sainabou Jobe's home.

We started going out together and very soon I had the courage to ask her hand in marriage. There was no bone of contention with regards for my love for her. She was the darling of my heart at first sight and I was not going to let a fly land on her from that day onwards.

We had a simple wedding because her father did not quite approve of me because of fear for his uneducated but very pretty daughter being dump at one stage of the marriage for another educated city girl.

I, in the long run, allied his fears and he ended up being one of my best friends and confidants I had up to the day he went to his maker. Fatou Koma-Ceesay and I are blessed with three beautiful daughters namely, Princesses Famatanding Ceesay, Binta Ceesay, and Roheyata Ceesay. All of who, unlike me, had their schooling start at the age of five.

The elder girl is aspiring to become a doctor and had been admitted to start her premed courses at Alpena Community College in Alpena, Michigan, USA.

Son of the Savannah

Together Fatou Koma-Ceesay, the children and I went through all the tragedy of hunger, poverty and other sad experiences my sojourn in the quest of the Golden flees for the villager brought to us. Fatou Koma-Ceesay initially hated Manding Medical Centre for she felt it consumed me and took me away from her and the children.

The call got me entangled in a web of unfortunate circumstances and laws. The marriage had at one point almost spiraled to its end as wife' move became questionable. Nonetheless she remained a good mother and wife who took care of the girls in my absence.

My mother in-law was battered by confusion and as to why Fatou stuck it out with me under such immense hardship. Love is stronger glue! We loved each other and so we were able to stand by the other in good or bad times and my trip to England was the worst ever in our connubial life.

It caused great turbulences in the marriage but I stuck with it for love's shake and the children who I love dearly. Today, we are back together as family under the same roof while planning and supporting future of our darling girls.

God bless Fatou Koma-Ceesay's heart and be reassured of endless love I have for her. For now Dalliance said it best for me when he said, "Say of me what you will and the morrow will judge you, and your words shall be a witness before its judgment and a testimony before it justice.

Dr. Alhasan Sisawo Ceesay, MD

I came to say a word and I shall utter it. Should death take me ere I give voice; the morrow shall utter it. That which alone I do today shall be proclaimed before the people in days to come." I wrote with the hope the life enshrined herein will serve not only as an inspiration to the despondent but a lesson never to allow this sort of experience it passed through this planet.

I wrote in the hope that life enshrined in my books will serve not only as an inspiration to the despondent and downtrodden but a lesson never to allow this sort of experience it passed through this planet.

I wrote because I felt that my life has something worth revealing to the world to engender tolerance and understanding between people and their governments.

I risked revealing today for all of us to learn from it and move to a better and rewarding future.

Among the forces of life is one that stands a certain lofty peak a few is endowed with or able to explore its heights. Ambition urges us to leave the lower surface of earth where the ordinary people live and ascend to heights that pierce the heavens.

This mission has led to numerous Erie paths but for me this Pell-mell towards a better medical service for the neglected villager was a worthwhile adventure. I am profoundly grateful and indebted to my wife Fatou Koma-Ceesay and our daughters, princesses Famatanding Ceesay, Binta Ceesay and Roheyata Ceesay for enduring all the pains that we went through in thick and thin times during my sojourn to America and England.

Also my deepest gratitude goes to Cousin Yata Sey-Corr for helping keep my family hopeful. God bless her heart eternally. I forgive my own brothers and sisters who refused to cater for my family in my absence. Hello, hats off to Sey kunda!

Dr. Alhasan Ceesay, holding Africa

Dr. Alhasan Sisawo Ceesay, MD
Chapter 18

MY ENDEARING LIFE & FATE

For a while in my native innocence all I had was erudition and wit, which always misfired. Everything I touched came to nothing but failure, whatever I tried to achieve came crashing down on my head.

At any given moment some mishap befalls me and nothing surprised me anymore. I took my current plight with stride and smiled as fate taunts me. I remain poor but my in extinguishable strong will enabled me face life squarely and took me through these dark days.

The twist of fate abated but my age had advanced beyond retrieval. The above apocalyptic life is indeed trying moments for my family and me. The only passion I have is providing medical service to villagers through Manding Medical Centre.

My dream spawns better future health service for future generations. I never set to write a bestseller but to inform and share ideas. Also I enjoy reading it as it's not found in any bookstore.

It is hoped that in writing another will be spared of experienced I endured before being able to provide medical service/aid to Gambian villagers. Browse: http://friendsofmandinggambimed.btck.co.uk or contact alhasanceesay@hotmail.com

To view/purchase books: Google search Dr. Alhasan Ceesay/ books.

Son of the Savannah

Dr. Alhasan S. Ceesay, MD

Chapter 19

THE WAY OF

A DREAMER

Back in the Gambia a friend decried my efforts as nothing but a dream that I persistently chased. I let such observers know that it only takes time before my dream become fruitful.

Here are a few examples: I left the Gambia in 1967 as a nurse and returned; after insurmountable roadblocks as a medical doctor. While practicing in the Gambia I further created two worthy entities, namely:

(1) The Gambia Health Credit Union, which today provides needed financial assistance to all health workers i.e. Nurses and Health Inspectors country wide.

(2) In addition I created NGO Manding Medical Centre at Njawara village, Lower Badibou to help provide a much needed medical aid and service free of charge to villagers who could not afford to pay private clinics. With the help of visiting doctors the centre has treated more than 9000 villagers free of charge since its inception in 1993.

On returning to the UK, I again with help of resident nurses and doctors in Colchester Essex setup the Friends of Manding Charitable trust in Colchester UK. This was recognized and registered as a charity in England and Wales by the UK- charity Commission in 2002.

In the midst of which I published my first book 'The Legend Against all Odds' and now has published more than thirty eight novels. To further cement my goal for the villager I was able to convince the Alpena City Council to form a sister city link with Njawara and Kinte Kunda villages in the Lower Badibous of the Gambia in 2005.

This was made easier after my being awarded on May 5th, 2005 'Distinguished Graduate Award' by Alpena Community College. My web site: friends of Manding gambimed continues to lure people to Njawara to see what help they could give the villager.

Today, I am not only an author of several books; Google search: Dr. Alhasan Ceesay/books to view of purchase as contribution to rural healthcare; portions or sales from these books go to support goals of Manding medical Centre at Njawara. I am indeed a dreamer and will continue to dream fir my people.

If the above is dream then here is another step to help see through me. I am humble to let you know I am now a Publisher and my company in the UK is 'PUBLISH KUNSA LTD' and one can have their work published by logging on to our web site; www.publishkunsa.com .

Again two pounds sterling from any book published by my company goes towards scholarships and rural healthcare as stipulated in terms of contract we would work on manuscripts. Dreams must be activated and not wasted.

Dr. Alhasan Sisawo Ceesay, MD

I cannot fly without wing but can make artificial wings to let reach higher hits that loafers never can dream of. Allow the dream to force you into action. Yes, I too have a dream, which is simply that every hamlet in the Gambia be bequeathed good healthcare, safe drinking water, enough food and chance to a solid education for every child.

Yes. Education is power and a mover. I sacrificed my life to endure depravity, humiliation and solitude in other to bring medical aid to villagers. With all these I am busy trying to get more medical skills and experience before heading to Gambia, home , sweet home.

With this tit-bit I can freely and willingly encourage you to dream but not to let it remain at that. A life with trials or challenge is like an orchestra without conductor and it very defeating if not boring indeed. One must act for the good of self and any community we find ourselves.

An old village sage once advice that 'A good person and at best a leader never yield to failure but only learns from it to move forward. Grand Pa Bajoja Ceesay told me that; "One willing to do good should not expect people to remove obstacles or stones from their path; but such leaders must accept it calmly in the event these place more boulders on our way."

This is what a dream turns out. At first it becomes a lonely avenue full of heartaches, which eases gradually as the good things unfold from one's relentless efforts to make the dream becomes fruitful and rewarding.. Simple its life 99.9% very hard work full of stumbling. Do not we all dream of going to heaven? Well the path to such respites need challenging theological and spiritual discipline. Hence we earthly dreamers dabble with ideas of landing on Mars and eventually colonizing it. So allow me ask, what is your dream for mankind, especially Africa?

Can Africa ever be free of ignorance, self subtenant, corruption and misuse of the tribe? These just few multipronged toxic dragon heads African must dream to remove from our midst. With better education and discipline Africa can overcome and progress. Dreamers are doing utmost to slay the pestilent dragon hindering life in the villages of rural Africa.

We must remove the monster of retro ration for the shake of the future generation. Again grandpa Bajoja Ceesay advices that we stay the good cause and never be taken by detractions. I am no millionaire but have a million dreams worthy of pursuing for my people. Would you dream along with me? Glad to let you know hard work yields rewarding fruits.

Dream and be in control of not only your own life but be a source of hope and inspiration while contributing positively to your community. Do not be carried along by current get rich quick and live selfishly. Life is to be shared even with dreamers.

Dr. Alhasan Sisawo Ceesay, MD

Time is not mine and life will continue for the villager. Success comes slowly and brings with it contagious hope that serves as blue print for other. The fate of mankind is up to each of us. Do not succumb to idleness.

Use youthful opportunity to develop out of ignorance, and corruption by having courage to bring change to the people. Be the change you want in others. Expect resistance on your path to bring change. A useful proxy in fulfilling a dream is not letting it wane away. Always think it possible and work hard at its realization.

Be warned to think what could be done and not that which cannot be archived. Matrix of success lies in hard work with guided ski full knowledge. I will work on my dream and morrow will be my judge along with benefits accrued from it.

I hope my last footprints of my journey on earth will inspire people towards doing well and sharing their worth with others. From one villager to another may this wish be true for rural Gambia.

Chapter 20

ABOUT THE AUTHOR

I was born at Njawara Village, Lower Badibou District in the North Bank of the Gambia. I am a scion of a Mandinka and Fulani tribe and am one of five siblings. I had my education at Kinte Kunda, then Armitage High School, ending up as a registered nurse at the Royal Victoria Hospital, Banjul, before embarking to the USA on my medical degree quest.

I graduated from the American University School of Medicine in Montserrat, West Indies, in 1992 and returned to the Gambia to start setting up a self-help village health NGO Manding Medical Centre.

The Gambia Government and the Badibou local authority register NGO Manding Medical Centre. The centre has treated more than 9000 patients free.

I am married to Fatou Koma-Ceesay and we are blessed with three beautiful girls, Famatanding Ceesay, Binta Ceesay and Roheyata Ceesay. Unlike me, all of them started school early without the roadblocks I had to cross in my early years. I am currently a medical officer at the Royal at the Royal Victoria Hospital on study leave.

Dr. Alhasan Sisawo Ceesay, MD

It is my hope that this work will inspire others and bring much needy help to providing medical service to rural Gambia. You are urged to log onto:

www.friendsofmandinggambimed.btck.co.uk , to learn more about my work with villagers. Dear reader I hope you enjoyed navigating through the piece of work I am contribute for all of us makes case for change in attitudes of government and the governed. For now, Dalliance said it best for me when he said, "Say of me what you will and the morrow will judge you, and your words shall be a witness before its judgment and a testimony before its justice. I came to say a word and I shall utter it. Should death take me ere I give voice, the morrow shall utter it. That which alone I do today shall be proclaimed before the people in days to come." I wrote with the hope the life and position enshrined herein will serve as not only an inspiration to farmers, the despondent but also a lesson never to allow these shameful international jigsaw games continue as experience to pass through this planet. I felt that it is worth writing about the above because it is something worth revealing to honourable men and women to engender change, tolerance and understanding between people and governments. I risked speaking out for all of us to learn from it and move forward to a better and rewarding future.

Mission

Our objective is to improve the healthcare delivery to villagers, educating youths on STD and Drugs and quality of life for the people in rural Gambia. The Manding Medical Centre strives to accomplish this goal through primary health care and disease prevention, the promotion of health policy, health research and increased access to health care education for the people in the Gambia.

Have your manuscript become a book by submitting it for possible publication to acquisitions publishes Kunsa. Com

Please contact us to expose your work globally.

PUBLISH KUNSA.COM

Why Publish Kunsa?

At Publish Kunsa.com writers can get published free of all common hassles from soft paperbacks, hard cover to e-book versions.

 Easy to Publish
Etiam ullamcorper. Suspendisse a pell entesque dui, non felis.

Leave a Legacy
Etiam ullamcorper. Suspendisse a pell entesque dui, non felis.

 Scholarships
Etiam ullamcorper. Suspendisse a pell entesque dui, non felis.

 Worldwide Distribution
Etiam ullamcorper. Suspendisse a pell entesque dui, non felis.

 Donate
Etiam ullamcorper. Suspendisse a pell entesque dui, non felis.

 Excellent Support
Etiam ullamcorper. Suspendisse a pell entesque dui, non felis.

More about Publish Kunsa

Web design by Samson Web Design

GAMBIA HAS DECIDED TO BE FREE: PRESIDENT ADAMA BARO WHEELNG YAHYA JAMMEH TO EXILE IN GUINEA EQUITORIAL JANUARY 2017